Sabers, Sails, and Murder

Nola Robertson

Also by Nola Robertson

Tarron Hunter Series

Hunter Bound
Hunter Enslaved
Hunter Unchained
Hunter Forbidden
Hunter Scorned
Hunter Avenged

Also Available

Stolen Surrender

St. Claire Witches

Hexed by Fire
Spelled With Charms

A Cumberpatch Cove Mystery

Death and Doubloons
Sabers, Sails, and Murder

CHAPTER ONE

"Maxwell, what's up with this sword?" Grams, the nickname I used for Abigail Spencer, my grandmother, bellowed from the bottom of the stairs leading to the storage area below deck on the *Buccaneer's Delight*. The boat belonged to her son and my uncle Max who ran one of several local pirate tours from the docks near the Cumberpatch Cove harbor.

He liked to make the trips fun for the children and had recently added birthday parties to the list of activities he offered. Since I managed and ordered all the items sold at Mysterious Baubles, my family's shop, I'd also been tasked with providing all his supplies.

Grams and I had arrived a half-hour earlier to restock the face painting kits and miniature chests he now included in all his treasure hunts. Instead of my purse and the empty box I'd expected her to be carrying when she reappeared at the top of the stairs, she had a sword and swished it through the air as if she were a practiced swordsman or woman in her case. When she came close to catching the end of her ankle-length plaid skirt, I worried she might hurt herself.

"Where did you find the sword?" I took a step back to

avoid another swipe. "Maybe you should think about putting it back wherever you found it."

"It's actually a pirate saber." My uncle set the plastic garbage bag he'd used to gather discarded advertising brochures, empty drink containers, and snack wrappers left over from his previous tour near his feet, then pulled the drawstring.

Max Spencer was tall, burly, and had the same hazel eyes as Grams. His uniform, a pirate costume complete with a feather plume sticking out of his hat, was as good as or even better than anything found in a major motion picture. He'd also grown a short beard to make his outfit seem more authentic. On the rare occasion when he wanted to annoy my grandmother, he'd threatened to grow it out and have me braid it for him.

"I bought it over at the Booty Bazaar on Sea Biscuit Avenue." Max scratched his chin. "Supposedly, it belonged to Martin Cumberpatch. The salesclerk said they bought it from old Clyde Anderson. He wanted to get rid of it because he swears it's haunted."

Clyde was the caretaker at the By the Bay Cemetery, one of our local tourist attractions. You didn't grow up in this area of Maine without hearing stories about how the not so famous pirate our town was named after haunted the graveyard, supposedly searching for buried treasure.

My entire family and most of the town believed in any paranormal, supernatural, or magical entity ever written about. The ghost of our community's legendary pirate was at the top of everyone's list.

I'd never seen him and believed the rumors had been generated to encourage more business. Hearing the saber was haunted should have been reason enough not to buy it, and would have been for me. Unfortunately, the other members of my family believed otherwise. Any item given an otherworldly label automatically guaranteed a sale.

"Really?" Grams stopped the saber mid-swish so she could examine the blade more closely. "Have you showed it to Jonathan yet?"

Jonathan was my father, Max's younger brother, and out of all my relatives, his quest for anything supernatural bordered on obsessive. I didn't think there was a haunted house anywhere in the entire state he hadn't toured at least once, including the five he'd dragged me along to visit. If the saber belonged to Martin, and there was a possibility he'd get to see the pirate's ghost, then he'd definitely be interested.

"Of course, I did." Max rolled his eyes as if the answer should have been obvious. "I even had it authenticated. It was made in the seventeen hundreds, but they weren't able to prove whether or not it belonged to Martin."

"Well, that's too bad," Grams said.

"Yeah, but even if it wasn't Martin's, it adds quite a bit of realism to the tour, don't you think?" Max grinned.

Realism or not, I'd feel a lot better if he kept it out of my grandmother's hands. "Shouldn't you keep it locked up or something? You know, to make sure no children get a hold of it." I cringed when Grams took another swipe and mentally amended my thought on the subject to include older adults who should know better.

"I always keep it inside there." He tipped his chin at the beautiful wall-mounted case with a dark wooden frame and glass door behind us. Inside there were several other pirate artifacts and an empty spot with two hooks where I assumed the saber should have been.

I glanced back at my uncle. "Don't you keep the case locked?" Max had always been safety-minded, so I couldn't believe he hadn't taken precautions to protect his customers.

"I do, but somehow the darned thing finds a way out without any help. Now and then, I'll find it in the strangest places." He stared reflectively at the doorway behind Grams. "One time, I even found it in the spare bunk in the room below that I occasionally use as an office."

I glanced between the two of them. "Does anyone

besides me think that's a little creepy?" I knew better than to ask, but couldn't help myself.

Grams smiled and stopped swinging. "If this did belong to Martin, then maybe it's his ghost that keeps removing it from the case."

Because of my own recent ghostly experience where my friends and I ended up helping Jessica, my tour guide friend who'd been murdered, find her hereafter, I knew ghosts were real. My beliefs about the spirit world might have been swayed, but it didn't mean I believed a three-hundred-year-old ghost was haunting my uncle's boat any more than I thought werewolves and vampires existed. At least I wouldn't think they were real until I'd seen one with my own eyes.

Since I'd seen Jessica's ghost walk through a fence, I had a hard time accepting the fact that a spirit was capable of actually moving solid objects rather than passing through them. I narrowed my gaze at the round metal lock securing the glass door on the left side of the frame. "Without the key?"

Grams shook her head and tsked, dismissing my suggestion that the laws of physics applied to the situation. I braced, sure that she was about to give my uncle and me another one of her psychic revelations.

The last one occurred a few months ago and involved a mouse who would sneak into my office at the shop and steal tidbits of my breakfast muffins. Supposedly, the rodent was the reincarnation of my great-great-uncle Howard and made a habit of showing up whenever a member of my family needed help. If I remembered correctly, the time before that, he'd shown up in the form of a hamster.

Even though the furry creature had inadvertently helped me find the clue that led my friends and me to Jessica's killer, I still had my doubts we were related.

"The key never leaves the ring." Max reached into his pants pocket and dangled the proof in front of me.

Since Grams had added jabs and fancy footwork to her swordplay, and I preferred not to be headline news should one of us end up skewed, I decided to use the one thing that might persuade her to hand over the weapon.

"If the saber is haunted, do you think the owner will be upset that you're using it?"

Grams widened her eyes and stopped swiping, then glanced around as if she expected Martin to appear magically. "Oooh, you could be right. Maybe we should put it back. Besides, I'm supposed to meet with Nadine when we finish so I can help her finalize plans for this year's fortune teller booth."

The residents of Cumberpatch were big on celebrating everything. Next to the Founders Day celebration, the pirate festival scheduled for the upcoming weekend was the town's biggest annual event. The booth Grams was helping Nadine with was one of many attractions that would be available for the influx of tourists who'd be arriving for the festivities.

"I think that sounds like a good idea." Max stepped closer to the display case and slipped the key in the lock.

Glad I finally had my uncle's support, I held my hand out to Grams, then wiggled my fingers hoping she'd turn over the blade so I wouldn't have to wrestle it away from her.

Reluctantly, and after swinging at an imaginary opponent one more time, she handed me the weapon. The instant I gripped the metal hilt, I received an electrical shock. Only it wasn't a regular jolt, or anything close to what a person would expect if they'd accidentally touched a household outlet. No, this was a full-blown zap with enough power to send a painful shock that ran from my wrist to my elbow.

At the same time, I released an embarrassingly girly squeal and tossed the saber. Luckily, when the blade sailed through the air and made its dissent, it missed Grams and Max before landing on the deck with a clank.

Max was the first to reach me and placed a hand on my shoulder. "Rylee, are you okay?"

I struggled with nausea, and my fingers tingled. What I wanted to do was shake my head and scream that I wasn't all right, but I didn't want him to worry, or hover. Max had never married and didn't have any children, so being his only niece had always earned me his fatherly affections. "I'm fine. It was only a shock."

There wasn't anything normal about the electrical jolt. The residual ache in my hand and arm felt the same way they did after I'd been zapped by the spirit seeker. Only on that particular occasion, I'd made the mistake of opening what I'd thought was a uniquely designed box of chocolates, which turned out to be a magical object my father had sent me as a birthday present.

I didn't like thinking about the blue tendrils that had wrapped me in a cocoon and given me the ability to see and interact with a spirit. An ability I'd hoped would disappear like Jessica had when she'd gone to the otherworldly realm.

I wasn't willing to repeat what had just happened and flexed my fingers, then glared at the offensive piece of metal as if it were a venomous snake.

"Are you sure?" The disbelief I heard in Gram's concerned voice was understandable. She was the one who found me passed out on the floor of my office after the last time I'd been zapped.

I nodded, then cringed when Max walked over and reached for the saber. "Maybe you shouldn't…"

He gripped the handle the same way I had, even running his fingertip along the smooth, flat surface of the blade. "Seems to be okay now." He offered me a weak smile, then headed for the case. "I'll lock this up, then walk you back to your car."

Usually, I wouldn't let him get away with being so overprotective, but at the moment, I didn't mind.

Max didn't know about my previous incident, so it was

no surprise when Grams cast me a look that said we'd be discussing what had happened later. "If you're sure you'll be okay, then I guess I'm off to see Nadine." With a wave of her hand, she headed across the deck. She'd made it as far as the ramp leading to the walkway below, had her hand on the white handrail before jerking to a stop. "Uh, Max."

"Yeah." He finished twisting the lock into place before turning to face her.

"You might want to get over here. It looks like Jake is standing outside your shop and handing out tickets or something to your customers."

Max rushed to the railing and peered over the side, then groaned. "That man is unbelievable." He stomped across the deck, pausing long enough for Grams to move out of the way. After a conspiratorial glance in my direction, she hastened to follow him the remainder of the way down the ramp.

The rivalry between Jake Durant, owner of the Sea Witch Pirate Tours, and Max had been going on for several years. Jake was my uncle's biggest competitor, and his unethical business practices had been a topic of discussion at more than one Spencer family get together.

Max rarely got angry unless provoked, which lately Jake seemed to do quite regularly. With Grams getting involved, I had a feeling things were about to escalate and decided my intervention might be needed.

I hurried down the stairs to the small room Max used as an office and grabbed my purse and the empty box. The minute I returned to the top of the stairs, a brisk chill swept across my body, cold enough to give me goosebumps. Even though we'd said our good-byes four months ago, anytime my skin prickled from a freezing sensation, I expected Jessica's ghost to appear wearing one of her odd hats that seemed to change colors with her moods.

I had no idea what had caused the drastic change in

temperature. It was a sunny day, not the slightest hint of a breeze. A few random clouds sprinkled the blue skies, the surrounding water was calm, the surface barely showing any ripples.

Shaking off my trepidation, I secured the door behind me and started across the deck. A movement to my left caught my attention, and I glanced at the six water cannons painted in brilliant blue and mounted along the railing. Max had installed them to keep the kids busy during the tour, but I'd seen quite a few adults having just as much fun as they tried to see how far they could shoot a stream of water.

Luckily, the swivel underneath was designed to keep the cannons from moving very far in either direction; otherwise, quite a few of Max's passengers would have gotten soaked by the mischievous antics of their children.

Standing next to the cannon at the far end was a man dressed in a pirate outfit. He was wearing a hat similar to my uncle's; only his didn't have a colorful feather sticking out of the brim. I thought I knew all of Max's employees, and I was sure he wasn't one of them.

Though it did seem a little early to be wearing a costume, it wasn't uncommon for tourists to dress up like Martin for the festival. Maybe this was one of those guys who enjoyed role-playing.

It was late afternoon, and as far as I knew, the last tour of the day had ended about a half-hour or so before Grams and I had arrived. There was no reason for him to be on the boat, and there most certainly wasn't a reason for him to have his hand on the trigger. He aimed and fired, his laughter filling the air after the people standing on the dock below had gotten drenched and started squealing.

"Hey, what do you think you're doing? Those aren't toys." I pointed at the cannon too late to stop another pulse of water to shoot through the air.

I tightened my grip on my purse strap and walked

toward him. "You need to stop right now before you hurt somebody." The causing pain part of my statement wasn't exactly the truth. When I was younger, my best friends Jade, Shawna, and I used to play with the cannons. I knew the water coming out of the barrel had the same pressure as a water hose. It wouldn't hurt unless you received a blast in the face.

He jerked his head in my direction, surprise glinting in his dark eyes. He glanced around as if he thought I was talking to someone else. When he finally realized I was glaring at him, he removed his hand from the trigger. "Ye can see me?"

"Of course, I can see you. It's not like you're trying to hide or anything." I was pretty sure the victims of his prank could see him too. "I know the owner of this boat. He's not going to be happy with you either."

I set the box down, then leaned over the railing so I could assess the damage myself. Grams was nowhere in sight, but Max and Jake, along with a group of five tourists were standing in and around a large puddle of water. Several people, those closest to my uncle and Jake, had received the brunt of the blast. Their clothes were soaked, their colorful T-shirts plastered to their skin. All of them glared at me instead of the culprit responsible for drenching them, even the people who had only gotten a light spraying.

Max took off his hat, his glare shooting from his no longer pluming feather to me. "Rylee, what the heck?"

"I didn't do it, he did." I hitched my thumb at the pirate guy.

"He who? There's nobody there," Jake growled as he wiped the water off his bald head, then shook off the excess water.

"Hey, don't yell at my niece." Max coming to my defense wouldn't last long and wasn't going to keep me from getting a lecture later. While he and Jake argued, the crowd had sense enough to move outside the spray zone and continued mumbling their disapproval of what they thought I'd done.

I was no longer in any hurry to leave the boat and decided to give the pirate guy a piece of my mind for starting this whole fiasco. He was still standing near the railing, making Jake's comment about not being able to see him even more confusing.

As if his smirk hadn't been irritating enough, he smugly crossed his arms and quirked a brow as if chastising him further wasn't going to do any good. When he faded into nothingness, then reappeared five feet away from me, my annoyance turned to shock. My comprehension of the situation, the reason he'd asked me if I could see him, and why no one else could, finally made sense.

Another ghost was haunting me.

"No, no, no," I muttered. My knees no longer wanted to cooperate, and I grabbed for the railing between the two closest cannons to keep my rear from ending up on the hardwood deck beneath my feet.

Was it possible I still had lingering effects from the spirit seeker, that somehow the shock I'd received from touching the saber had enabled me to see his ghost? Or was it possible that I'd pulled spirits from the afterlife, and would have to spend the rest of my life being careful what I touched?

The thought of Cumberpatch overrun with spirits made my chest tighten and had me gulping air.

As much as I avoided visiting the Classic Broom because of its scary interior and even spookier shop owners, I would need to make an exception and talk to the Haverston sisters again. Edith and Joyce had provided me with some answers shortly after my encounter with the spirit seeker. They were the only people I knew of who might be able to help me now.

Even though I had my suspicions about the identity of the guy who'd just gotten me into trouble, I needed to be sure.

"Are ye all right, Lass? Ye look as if ye have seen…well, me." He chuckled heartily.

Great, not only was I being haunted again, but this ghost liked to play tricks and found himself amusing. "My name is Rylee, not Lass. And speaking of names, would you mind telling me yours?"

He removed his hat, then made an exaggerated bow. "I be Martin Cumberpatch, cap'n of the *Renegade's Revenge*. 'Ave ye heard of me?"

My excitement overruled my irritation. "Are you kidding? The town was named after you." I tugged the strap of my purse back onto my shoulder. "I don't think there's anyone in the state who doesn't know who you are. I just never expected to actually meet you, or be standing here talking to you." Though I didn't think haphazardly leaning on a water cannon could be considered standing.

He puffed out his chest and proudly grinned throughout my rambling.

I narrowed my eyes. "But you already knew that, didn't you?"

"Aye."

Curiosity and I were best friends, so when I could finally take a step without fear of falling, I moved closer to get a better look at Martin. "Not to be rude or anything, but do you mind if I touch you?"

"Nah at all." He seemed to be enjoying our encounter way more than I was and took a few steps closer.

"Shouldn't you be blue?" Except for the different hats that changed colors, Jessica's ghost had always shimmered a single translucent shade. I waved my arm through the air, ignoring the chill I got when my hand passed through his chest. "And glowing. Why aren't you glowing? Did something happen, and you didn't get to cross over?" I wasn't an expert on all things ghostly, but I had it on decent advice that moving onto the afterlife was a spirit's primary goal.

"Nah, I be likin' it here jus' fine." Martin's grin faltered slightly.

"But why?" His revelation was not what I'd expected, and if I wanted to hurry him on his way, I'd need more information. "Don't you want to be with your crew?" I assumed since they weren't hanging out with him, they must have passed on.

"What makes ye reckon I be wantin' to spend eternity wit' that scurvy lot?" He huffed. "They were nah much fun when they were alive, always wantin' to plunder, drinkin' too much ail, and searchin' fer treasure." His reflective look when he mentioned the latter made me wonder if it meant something personal to him.

It was hard to tell if he was being serious or trying to be humorous. Before I could ask, heavy footsteps on the ramp filled the air along with Max's voice. "Rylee." It hadn't reached the level of a shout but was loud enough to get my attention. My uncle's arrival didn't go unnoticed by Martin, either. The cowardly pirate vanished, leaving me to deal with my irate relative alone.

"Yeah," I said, pushing away from the railing. By the time Max reached the top of the ramp, he didn't look nearly as angry as I'd expected.

He crossed the deck, stopping a few feet away from me, then placed his hands on his hips. "Girl, I don't know what possessed you to spray us with water, but…"

"I can explain." I wasn't willing to tell him about Martin's ghost and had already formulated an excuse about the water shooting being an accident or the result of a malfunctioning cannon.

"No need." Max grinned, then pulled me into a breath-stealing soggy hug. "I wanted to say thank you."

I narrowed my gaze, afraid I'd been wrong about the strength of the blast, that the water had hit him in the head and caused some damage. "Thank you for what?"

"For doing to Jake what I've wanted to do for years."

CHAPTER TWO

"No way, Martin Cumberpatch, really?" Shawna plopped down next to me on the couch in the living room of the apartment she shared with Jade.

Her reaction was pretty much what I'd expected after sharing the details of my encounter with the feisty pirate.

"Does he look anything like the pictures in our high school history books?" She tucked several dark brown strands streaked with vibrant blue behind both ears.

I had gotten used to the bright purple streaks she'd been wearing since the beginning of summer. Apparently, she'd decided it was time to change after finding out that shade of blue was Nate's favorite color.

He'd been Jessica's ex-boyfriend, and we'd met him, or rather Shawna had tackled him to the ground, the night we decided to break into the cemetery to revisit her crime scene for clues. The interaction between them always seemed strained, so I was surprised by her recent interest in the guy.

Jade and I had a bet going on whether or not they'd actually start dating. There wasn't any money involved because we agreed that if they did get together, the relationship would only last a few months, the break-up occurring right around the New Year.

"I'd say they're fairly accurate. Martin didn't glow, not like Jessica had, so at first, I thought he was a tourist."

"If he'd been trapped in this world all these years, maybe his spirit's luster faded." Jade shared her speculation as she handed me a mug of freshly brewed coffee before settling with her favorite teal cup in the cushioned chair across from us. She slipped off her shoes, then smoothed the fabric of her jeans as she tucked her legs beside her.

"It might also explain why he can move objects." Shawna tapped her chin, then answered my inquiring glance. "He's had lots of time to practice."

"I would say so," I said. "I still can't believe Martin shot Max and Jake with a water cannon."

Jade giggled. "I'll bet that went over well."

"Oh yeah." I bobbed my head. "Jake was furious, but surprisingly, Max was happy about it afterward. I guess he'd wanted to do it for years, or so he said." I didn't need to explain the feud between the two men to my friends. They'd spent a lot of time with my family and had heard plenty of my uncle's rants.

"Did Martin happen to tell you why he was still hanging around?" Shawna reached for the cup she had sitting on the coffee table in front of her.

"He said something about not wanting to spend eternity with his crew, but I got the impression he might be joking." I took a sip of my drink. "I didn't get a chance to ask him anything else because he poofed out when Max came on the boat."

"I take it you haven't seen him since yesterday, then?" Shawna asked.

"No." I kept the part about hoping I wouldn't see him again to myself. It might be selfish, but I wasn't looking forward to my life being complicated by a ghost again.

"Do you think he can do that pop in and out thing that Jessica used to do?" Jade asked.

"More importantly, do you think Martin will show up here?" Shawna excitedly glanced around the room as if the ghost would magically appear at the mention of his name.

"No, and I hope not." I sighed, glancing at both of them in turn.

"Oooh, you know what this means, don't you?" Shawna asked.

"That I'm cursed." My sarcasm sounded harsher than I'd intended.

"Nooo." Shawna rolled her eyes. "It means you're destined to help ghosts in need."

"Great, so now you think the spirit seeker made me some sort of beacon for ghosts in trouble." If I was a magical guiding light, then finding out for sure was another reason I needed to visit the Haverston sisters. And soon.

"Exactly, which is why we need to find out why Martin's here so we can help him like we did Jessica," Shawna said.

"Martin didn't seem like he wanted any help." Going out and purposely looking for another sleuthing adventure was definitely not on my to-do list, especially now that my life had returned to what I considered to be as normal as it was going to get.

"Did you ask him, or even offer your services?" Jade asked.

"What services?"

Shawna joined Jade in staring at me as if it was obvious, pausing a few seconds before saying, "You know, the spirit whisperer thing."

Even if being a ghost whisperer was a legitimate profession, I was sure it wouldn't look good on my resume, or assist with paying my bills.

Shawna patting the armrest and staring off into space made me nervous because it usually meant she was devising a plan that would get us into trouble. "Max's first tour doesn't usually leave until eleven in the morning, right?"

"As far as I know." A tightening in my chest compounded my wariness.

"Then I say we go down to the *Buccaneer's Delight* to see if Martin is still there and find out why he hasn't moved on yet," Shawna said.

"I think it's a great idea." Jade shot Shawna a supportive grin.

"No, it's not a great idea," I said when Jade lowered her feet to the floor and reached for her shoes. "In fact, it's a bad idea. One ghost in my lifetime was enough, thank you." Since I hadn't seen Martin after our conversation the day before, I was hoping I'd gotten lucky, and there was some cosmic rule that kept him from leaving the boat. If that was the case, I already had plenty of excuses to tell my uncle why I'd be leaving my deliveries in his shop from now on.

"But Rylee, what if he really does need our help and was too proud to ask for it?" Shawna's pleading voice was getting close to whining.

"He's a pirate. You do remember the stories about pillaging and taking what they wanted, right?" If anything, I was more worried the locals would need some help protecting themselves from Martin and his prankster antics.

"Yes, but that doesn't mean we shouldn't at least discuss it with him," Jade said.

Glaring at my friends wasn't doing me any good. They were equally determined, and there was no way I was going to win a two against one battle of wills. "You're not going to stop pestering me until we go, are you?"

Jade shook her head. "Nope."

"Probably not," Shawna said.

"Fine. We'll go and ask your questions." I held up my hand. "But if he doesn't want our help, then that's the last time we go looking for him." I gave them both an unwavering glare.

Jade and Shawna glanced at each other, shared a smirk,

then said, "Agreed."

My friends were in a hurry to go and rushed around the apartment in search of jackets and whatever else they thought they needed to take with them. I drained the last of my drink, wishing I'd had time for at least two more cups of the caffeine-infused liquid before having to deal with Martin.

***

My family's shop, along with quite a few other businesses, was located on Swashbuckler Boulevard, the town's main street. Taking the road that circled through town was the quickest way to reach the harbor and Max's boat.

Weekends were usually the busiest, and in a few days, tourists would fill the sidewalks, and the traffic would be a lot heavier. After parking in one of the lots designated for the surrounding shopping areas, Shawna, Jade, and I decided to stop by Max's store first to make sure no one would be on the *Buccaneer's Delight* while we were looking for Martin.

Chloe Carter, one of my uncle's employees, was unlocking the door to the blue building where they sold a variety of souvenirs and tickets for the tours. There were several seagulls perched on the roof next to a long rectangular sign painted a bright yellow with the words "Pirate Cruises" in large red letters centered along the middle.

All of Max's employees were required to dress like pirates. Chloe's uniform consisted of a white blouse that gathered across the bodice, a long dark skirt with ruffles along the hem, and a matching vest with his company's logo.

As soon as she saw us, she waved. "Hey, Rylee, if you're looking for Max, he hasn't arrived yet, but I'm sure he'll be here shortly."

If Max and the other employees who worked the tour were due to arrive soon, it didn't give my friends and me much time to go onboard and find Martin.

"Thanks, but I only stopped by to pick up something I left below deck when I was here yesterday. If it's okay with you…" I motioned toward the boat.

"Not a problem. Go ahead, but please make sure you latch the rope at the bottom of the ramp when you're through." After shoving a plastic wedge under the door with her foot to keep it open, Chloe turned to go back inside.

Shawna only made it a few steps before asking, "What did you forget yesterday? I thought we came here to talk to Martin."

"Nothing," I whispered, heading along the concrete walkway leading to the boat.

"Then what was that all about?" Shawna asked.

"Covert operation, remember?" Jade latched onto Shawna's elbow and hurried her along so Chloe wouldn't overhear our conversation if she came back outside. "Did you expect Rylee to tell her we came here looking for a ghost? Because if she had, it wouldn't take long before everybody in town found out and was out here trying to find him."

"Not to mention the hounding I'd get if Troy Duncan ever found out." Troy was a local reporter who worked for his father's newspaper, the Swashbuckler Gazette. The last time I'd refused to be interviewed by him was at Jessica's crime scene. The last time there'd been a murder, which happened to be Jessica's, he'd hounded me for an interview at the cemetery.

Shawna was a thoughtful person whose consistent plan of helping others almost always landed the three of us in trouble. She was also notorious for losing sight of the goal and needed numerous reminders about the objective. "If that happens, we can forget about being able to help Martin."

"Good point." Shawna pulled free of Jade's hand to follow me up the ramp.

As soon as I reached the deck, I walked over to the area near the water cannons where I'd last seen Martin's ghost.

"Anything?" After glancing around, Jade pushed her blonde bangs off her forehead, then placed her sunglasses on top of her head.

I shook my head. "Nothing, not even a chill. Maybe what happened yesterday had been a fluke." Not that I believed it, but I could always hope.

Shawna did a slow spin. "It's been a while since I've been on board, but the boat hasn't changed a bit."

"Do you guys remember that summer we all worked on the tours with Max?" Jade asked.

Shawna wrinkled her nose. "Yes, and I also remember wanting to throw a kid over the railing for sticking bubblegum in my hair."

The child she'd mentioned was an eleven-year-old boy whose mother had let him and his friends run wild during the entire trip. He was a rambunctious brat who kept trying to lift my skirt, and I'd come close to helping Shawna fulfill her threat.

Jade bobbed her head. "I remember that too. Didn't I have to cut the chewed up wad out for you?"

"You tried, but I still ended up at the hairdresser's," Shawna said. It was the first and last time I ever wore my hair that short."

As much as I enjoyed reminiscing with my friends about our misadventures, I didn't want to be here when Max or any of his crew arrived to set up for the next tour.

"Martin, are you here?" I walked across the deck half-listening to Jade and Shawna's conversation wishing he'd hurry up and appear. I ended up in front of the display case, noticed the empty spot where I'd seen Max mount the saber, and groaned. "Unbelievable."

"What's the matter? What did you find?" Jade headed

in my direction, the click of her heels filling the air.

"It's not what I found." I tipped my chin at the empty spot behind the glass. "It's what's missing."

"Hey guys," Shawna interrupted before I got a chance to tell Jade I thought we should do a thorough search of the boat and find the artifact before we left, or at the very least, let Max know it had disappeared again.

Shawna leaned against the railing at the far end of the deck and was looking down at the water. Frowning, she glanced at us over her shoulder. "You know the sword thingy or whatever the heck it was that Max said he thought belonged to Martin?"

"You mean his saber?" Jade asked.

"Yeah, that." Shawna went back to staring at the water.

"Why?" I warily followed Jade to see what our friend was looking at, unsure if I was going to like what she had to say.

"Because I think I found it." Shawna leaned farther over the edge and pointed.

Since the surrounding water was deep and metal was too heavy to float, she wouldn't be able to see the blade if it sank to the darkened depths. I peered over the side, expecting to see the blade stuck somewhere in the wooden hull, not protruding from someone's chest.

My inhaled squeak was followed by a gasp when Jade took the spot next to me and got a glimpse of what Shawna found. "That's, that's…"

"A dead body," Shawna stated in a matter-of-fact tone.

This wasn't the first non-living person I'd seen, not that I had a history of finding bodies lying around. I'd been to Jessica's crime scene at the cemetery, and at the time, seeing blood covering the ground had seemed way worse and made me nauseous.

Even so, I couldn't stop staring at Jake Durant as he bobbed along with the incoming waves with my uncle's saber sticking out of his chest.

"Ahoy, Lass." Martin's cheery greeting and sudden

appearance unraveled the composure I'd mustered, along with any thoughts on how to deal with our discovery. If my system received any more shocks, I wasn't sure if I'd make it through the rest of the day.

I couldn't decide what was more startling; having him show up out of nowhere or that he was wearing jeans and a T-shirt with a Cumberpatch Cove logo stamped above the pocket on the left side of his chest.

If I hadn't been jumping several inches off the ground and making a noise somewhere between a guttural shriek and a gurgle, I might have thought to ask him how ghosts were able to change their wardrobe.

"Rylee, are you okay?" Since I hadn't announced the spirit's arrival, Jade had no doubt assumed my reaction was linked to finding Jake.

"Oooh, I've seen that look before. I'll bet Martin's here, isn't he?" Shawna grinned and glanced around, more interested in seeing our ghostly visitor than whether or not my heart was going to continue beating.

After a few deep breaths that helped slow my pulse, I was able to say "yes" in a semi-normal voice.

"Who be these pretty wenches?" Martin scratched his chin. "The one with the silky blonde hair be quite fetchin'."

"This is Jade and Shawna." I pointed at each of them in turn, then pinned him with a glare. "They're my best friends, and ogling them is off-limits." If I knew my hand wouldn't go all the way through his chest, I'd have poked him to show him I was serious.

Jade didn't have a problem being vocal if she knew a guy was leering at her, so I was glad my comment only received a raised brow.

"What ye be lookin' at?" Martin ignored my threat, then stepped closer to the railing and peered over. "Be that nah the bloke who had words with the owner of this fine galleon nah long ago?"

"That would be my uncle Max, and yes, it's the same

guy." I didn't believe he was the culprit, but I eyed him suspiciously anyway. "You wouldn't happen to know how he ended up that way, would you?"

Martin took my question as an insult and crossed his arms. "I be havin' no idea. Though I be wantin' to know who used me saber to run 'im through."

Max would be excited to hear his assumption about the blade's owner had been correct. It was too bad I couldn't tell him without explaining how I'd found out.

"So, just to be clear, you're telling me you're not responsible for what happened to Jake?"

"O' course nah. Wha' kind of pirate do ye take me fer?" Martin's skin might not be shimmering, but it still had a translucent quality; otherwise, I was certain I'd see a flush on his cheeks.

I returned his glare. "Since you're the first real pirate I've ever met and, according to everything I've read, running someone through happened a lot in your time."

Martin scowled. "Well, ye should nah always believe everythin' ye be readin', now should ye?"

It appeared as if Jade and Shawna were struggling to follow my conversation with Martin. "The saber in question belongs to Martin, but he swears he wasn't the one to…"

"Run him through," Jade finished for me. "Got it."

Shawna swept the back of her hand across her forehead. "Well, that's a relief. I'd have been royally bummed if Martin turned out to be a killer ghost."

Martin pursed his lips. "Yer friend does know that I be standin' right here, 'n can hear her, does she nah?"

"Uh-huh," I said.

"I know we came here to talk to Martin, but shouldn't we do something about Jake first?" Jade asked.

"Like what, fish him out of the water?" I was prepared to argue vehemently if either of them suggested going anywhere near the body.

"It's obvious he's dead, so I don't think a little more

time in the water is going to hurt him any. I say we leave him where he is and report the murder." Jade reached into her black leather purse and pulled out her cell phone.

"Martin can move objects, right?" Shawna glanced over the railing, then back at Jade and me, her gaze beaming.

I held up my hand when Martin groaned. "He can hear you, so ask your questions, and I'll give you his answers." I'd taken on the role of intermediary when we'd helped Jessica. Having to repeat everything got a little annoying, and I wasn't looking forward to it.

Fortunately, Jade and Shawna had gotten good at deducing what Martin said from hearing my side of the conversation, so I only needed to supply occasional details.

"Oh, yeah, right." Shawna turned in Martin's general direction. "What do you think about going down there and pushing Jake closer to the dock?"

If I didn't know any better, I'd swear Martin was related to Shawna. He'd mastered her are-you-serious look perfectly.

"And why would we want him to do that?" Jade waved her phone in Shawna's face.

Shawna placed her hands on her hips. "To take pictures and see if there any clues."

Apparently, helping solve Jessica's murder had somehow convinced my friend she was qualified to be a crime investigator.

"Tell yer friend they say it ain't a good idea to move the body," Martin said.

"Who are they, and how do you know that?" The notion didn't sound like something anyone from his time would say. The more he talked, the more I listened to how he said things, and the more I wanted to know. A few centuries had passed since his reported death, yet he was familiar with modern terminology.

Had he been hanging around in this world all that time, or could he access a revolving door to the spirit world?

"I be havin' the pleasure of watchin' those murder

investigation shows on one of them machines ye be callin' a television."

If he'd had access to a television, my next thought was whose, and was it possible he'd been haunting someone else? I immediately thought of Max's comment about Clyde.

It wouldn't be long before people started to arrive for the next tour, so questions would have to wait. "You'll be happy to know Martin also watches crime shows and suggests we leave Jake where he is." I turned to Jade. "I think you should go ahead and call the police."

"You wouldn't be agreeing with her just to keep that handsome detective of yours from getting upset if we disturb his crime scene, are you?" Shawna smirked.

Finding Jake's body was complicated enough without my friend trying to play matchmaker. "One, Logan is not *my* detective. And two, what crime scene? It's not like they can cordon off the area around the boat with their special yellow tape, or get much evidence from someone bobbing in the water."

Jade swiped the screen, no doubt scrolling through her extensive contact list. "Are you sure you wouldn't like to make the call? Isn't Logan's personal number on the card he left for you at the shop when he was investigating Jessica's death?"

Not interested in Jade's matchmaking attempts either, I narrowed my gaze. "No, the only number he gave me was for the station."

When I'd first met Logan, he'd been living in Bangor, and an investigation into a string of museum robberies had led him to our town. Shortly after catching Jessica's killers, he'd told me about his plans to relocate to Cumberpatch. He'd been gone nearly two months before returning to work for his uncle, Roy Dixon, who was also the sheriff.

Logan thought he'd be arriving sooner, but finalizing his cases hadn't gone as planned, a fact he'd shared on the phone when he'd called to let me know he was back in town. He'd made a point of teasing me about staying out of trouble while he'd been gone.

Now that my friends and I had found a body, I didn't think Logan was going to be quite so flippant about the situation, and I tried not to cringe when I heard Jade tell whoever had answered the phone that she wanted to report a murder.

CHAPTER THREE

When the blare of sirens announcing the arrival of law enforcement reached us, Martin vanished. If he was as familiar with crime shows as he'd stated, then he had to know what the sound meant. Though I wasn't sure why he'd left. It wasn't as if the police could arrest him for anything.

I wondered if he'd been telling me the truth when he said he didn't have anything to do with Jake's death. Was he feeling guilty or experiencing a conditioned response? Had the lawbreaking exploits of his past life influenced his decision to go?

"It sure didn't take them very long to get here." Shawna had been pacing the area in front of the ramp ever since Jade made her call.

Elliott Barnes, a deputy we'd all known since high school, was one of the first to arrive. "What are you guys doing here?" He scowled, then herded us to the opposite side of the deck and out of the way.

Shawna placed her hands on her hips and defiantly glared at him. "Uh, her uncle owns the boat."

He took his hat off long enough to push his bangs off his forehead. "I mean, this is a murder scene, and you shouldn't be here."

"We,"—I pointed at Jade, Shawna, and myself—"found the body."

"Oh, nobody told me that." He cleared his throat. "I'm going to need you to stay right here." He pointed at the deck, trying to appear important. "I'm sure someone will be along shortly to talk to you."

He rushed off before my friends and I had a chance to ask any questions. I was glad Elliott had moved us to the canopied area where there were several rows of benches. Besides not wanting to add any more images of Jake bobbing in the water to the collection I'd already mentally gathered, I was getting tired of standing and plopped down on the nearest seat.

Under the circumstances, I thought I was doing a pretty good job of remaining calm. Though wondering whether or not Logan was assigned to the case didn't help my stress any.

"Sounds like this is going to take a while." With an annoyed sigh, Shawna dropped down on my left.

"This wasn't exactly the adventure I'd imagined," Jade said, settling in the middle of the bench on my right.

Instead of pointing out how I'd objected to coming here in the first place, I watched the two other officers who'd accompanied Elliott cordon off the area on the walkway below with some of their special yellow tape.

The group of people who'd bought their tickets for the next tour seemed more interested in what the police were doing then having their trip canceled. Max still hadn't arrived, but I noticed Chloe standing with a guy near the doorway to the tour shop. He had his back to me so I couldn't see his face, but he was wearing a pirate's costume and was most likely another one of my uncle's employees.

"Since we have to wait, we could find out why Martin is here." Jade shifted her purse, so it was sitting on her lap.

"We could if he hadn't already poofed out," I said.

"Well, that's too bad." Shawna got up on her knees,

then propped her elbows on the railing so she could get a better view of what was going on further down the walkway. "Maybe not," she said over her shoulder. "Especially after you see who is following Roy out of Max's shop."

The hint of mischief in the tone of her voice worried me, and my first thought was that the sheriff had brought Grams with him. The two of them had been friends forever. News traveled fast, and I was afraid she'd already heard about the tragedy. The muscles in my neck strained as I leaned to the side so I could see around Shawna.

I wasn't impressed by my friend's giggle or the way she was grinning after she'd caught me staring at Logan, not my grandmother.

Jade had gotten up to see who Shawna was talking about. "I agree." Her smirk was even more annoying than Shawna's.

I ignored my friends, doing my best not to show any interest in Logan's approach, yet unable to keep my gaze from straying in his direction. The last time I'd seen him was at the cemetery, and he'd been wearing jeans and a T-shirt. Today he was dressed professionally in a casual pair of black pants, a button-down shirt, and a tan jacket.

After slipping underneath the plastic tape, he continued toward the ramp leaving Roy to chat with Elliott and the other two officers.

As soon as he stepped on the deck, his dark whiskey eyes gravitated toward me. "Rylee, why am I not surprised to see you here?" Logan had a way of making even a scowl look attractive.

I knew better than to let my interest in the handsome detective distract me. I'd been through the investigation process with him once before. I'd even made the mistake of mentioning Jessica's name before he'd told me she'd been murdered. In my defense, I blurted out the information because I'd just seen her ghost, not that Logan was aware of my spirit communication ability.

"Hey, Logan." I wasn't good at playing dumb, and the since detective had a habit of twisting what I said to make me sound like a suspect, I decided the greeting would have to be sufficient.

If there was going to be an interrogation, it was interrupted by Max calling my name.

"Max, you can't go up there," Elliott said, stretching out his arms and rocking side to side, trying to keep my uncle from pushing his way up the ramp.

Max took another step closer and growled, "Elliott, unless you want to find yourself treading water, you will get out of the way and let me see my niece."

Roy had already come on board and was leaning against the railing, supervising his team while they removed Jake's body from the water. He frowned at the commotion. "It's okay, Barnes. Let him through."

Max stomped across the deck, the boards creaking under his weight. "I was on my way here when I got a call from Chloe telling me the police were all over the *Delight*, but she didn't tell me what happened?" His gaze jumped from Jade to Shawna, then back to me. "Are you girls all right?"

"We're fine, but Jake's not?" Jade said.

"What do you mean, Jake's not? What did he do now?" Max glanced around as if expecting to find the other man lurking about.

I placed my hand on his arm, then tipped my head toward the place where Roy was standing. "We found him in the water."

"Yep, somebody skewered him right through the chest with Mar…your saber." Shawna bobbed her head and mimicked a sharp blade piercing her heart.

"Shawna." Jade groaned and nudged her shoulder, then looked over at Roy to make sure they hadn't attracted his attention.

"What? He asked." Shawna shrugged. "It's not like our local law enforcement didn't already see it for themselves."

"Barnes, why don't you take a statement from these three," Logan pointed at Jade, Shawna, and Max in turn. "And once you're done, they can leave."

"What about Rylee?" Elliott asked.

"I'll take care of talking to her." Logan wiggled his index finger, motioning me away from the group. I wasn't sure why he was giving me special attention. His serious detective expression hadn't changed, and I was afraid he'd give me one of his lectures even though I hadn't done anything to deserve one. Though there was a good chance I'd earn one in the future if my decision to help Martin had anything to do with Jake's murder.

"We'll meet you back at the car when you're finished." Jade grinned, then tugged on Shawna's sleeve when it looked as if she might add a teasing comment.

With all the activity on and around the boat, the only other place left to go where we'd have privacy was below deck. Logan followed me down the stairs and into the cramped room Max sometimes used as an office.

Other than our one phone call, which was cut short, I hadn't seen or talked to him since he'd moved to Cumberpatch. Answering questions about a murder wasn't exactly how I'd envisioned spending time alone with him.

It seemed any personal questions I had weren't going to happen either, not if I was reading his intense gaze correctly.

He put some distance between us by crossing his arms and resting his backside on the edge of the desk. "I know I shouldn't have to tell you this, but after considering your penchant for doing what you want anyway, I'm going to caution you not to get involved."

It's not like I purposely searched for troublesome situations. I was pretty sure I wasn't going to like where our conversation was headed, so I leaned against the closest wall and mirrored Logan's body stance. "And why is that?"

"Because Max is a possible suspect."

I gasped. "You can't be serious. Why would you think my uncle, an outstanding member of the community, would commit murder?" I could feel the heat burning along my throat and cheeks. I wanted to argue that just because Max told Jake on more than one occasion that he'd end up as fish food if he didn't stop stealing his customers didn't mean my uncle had actually carried through on the threat. Hearing how incriminating it sounded in my head was enough to keep me from saying it out loud.

Logan pinched the bridge of his nose. "I didn't say I thought he committed the crime only that he is a suspect because you found Jake Durant's body near his boat."

"Yeah, well," I stammered. "Someone could have pushed Jake into the water anywhere along the pier, and the current could have pulled him in this direction."

"That's one possibility, but it doesn't explain how your uncle's saber found its way into the victim's chest. The display case where he keeps it is secured and shows no visible signs of damage." Logan held up his hand before I could come to Max's defense. "And two of your uncle's employees have already stated that he has the only key."

"Yeah, but…" I wanted to tell him the saber found its way out of the case on its own all the time, well maybe with a little assistance from a ghost. At this point, Martin being the owner was speculation since I hadn't gotten the chance to discuss the topic with him yet.

Sharing my theory with Logan would mean having to tell him about my ability. When he'd left for Bangor two months ago, he'd made it clear he was interested in getting to know me better. I was convinced if he found out about my ability, one I was determined to get rid of, it would ruin any chances of him ever asking me out. Chances that grew slimmer by the minute now that a member of my family was a possible suspect in his case.

"The last time you nearly…" He brushed his hand along my arm. "I just don't want to see anything bad

31

happen to you, okay?"

Surprised by his concern, my throat constricted, hindering any coherent response.

"I'd meant to give this to you before." He reached into his jacket pocket, retrieved a business card, then handed it to me. "My cell number is on the back."

"Thanks." I flipped the card over to see the ink scrawled numbers for myself.

"Logan," Elliott's panicked voice echoed from the stairwell. "You might want to get up here."

"Now what?" Logan snapped and hurried out of the room ahead of me.

Max, Shawna, and Jade were gone. Arlene Durant, Jake's wife, and Braden Wilkins, his business partner, had arrived during our absence.

"Sheriff Dixon, I insist you arrest Max Spencer immediately." Arlene stood in the middle of the deck, hands on her hips, her green eyes glaring at Roy. "Everyone knows he killed my poor, sweet Jake."

Her manicured nails were painted the same dark shade of pink as her tight-fitting floral dress. The only thing brighter than the flush on her cheeks was the crimson red she'd used to color her shoulder-length hair.

Did Arlene even know her husband? The man was neither poor nor sweet. He wasn't well-liked, at least not by my family, and I couldn't recall him ever having any close friends other than Braden.

I glanced between Roy and Logan, trying to determine whether or not they believed Arlene and were going to arrest my uncle.

"Come on, Arlene," Braden said as he wrapped his arm around Arlene's shoulder, which seemed a little bit more affectionate than supportive. "I'm sure the sheriff will do his job and find the killer."

"Fine." Arlene let Braden lead her to the ramp, but not before shooting a dirty look in my direction.

"Sorry about that, Rylee." I hoped the worried look on

Roy's face meant he was ignoring what Arlene had to say.

"No problem," I said. "Would it be all right if I left now?"

"Sure." He glanced towards Elliott. "I can have Barnes give you an escort if you like."

"No, I'm good." I headed for the ramp; my mind overwhelmed with thoughts.

Not only did I need to find out why Martin was here and help him back to the spirit realm, but with Arlene going around telling everybody she thought Max had murdered her husband, finding the real killer had now become a priority.

CHAPTER FOUR

The discussion Jade, Shawna, and I had after leaving Jake's crime scene lasted as long as it took us to drive to their place and left me with too many unanswered questions about his murder and my current dilemma with Martin.

Since Shawna had to work the dinner shift at the Cumberpatch Cove Cantina and Jade was headed off to have supper with her parents and her brother Bryce, I'd decided to stop by the shop and fill Grams in on what had happened. Or at least whatever she hadn't already heard via a call from Max.

I hadn't planned on working, but it turned out that my visit had been timely and great for business. The shop had an influx of customers, most of them locals, who'd heard the rumors about Max's involvement and were hoping to get an update from my family.

Grams was the gossip in the group, but she was also a shrewd businesswoman. She didn't have a problem sharing what she knew, which wasn't much, but not until those who were asking had purchased something first. The tidbits were passed along with large amounts of drama and included the psychic dream she'd had the night before, which she swore predicted a sinister event.

By the time I'd gotten home, it was late, I was exhausted, and the rest I'd needed had been minimal. I'd spent most of the night drifting in and out of sleep wondering who had wanted Jake dead, and realizing it was a long list. I might be able to narrow it down if I could figure out who might want my uncle Max to take the blame for it.

When I'd finally drifted off to the point where I could sleep, my imagination conjured a dream where Jake, not Martin, had returned as a ghost. The man was more insufferable in death than he was in life. Not only did I have to relive being accused of spraying him with a water cannon, but had been informed that he planned to haunt me until I found his murderer.

The fear of being stuck with Jake for any length of time jolted me from my unconscious state. With a groan, I rolled on my side and forced my eyes open, then was greeted by a furry face. "Morning, Barley." I scratched the head of the Kurilian Bobtail I'd inherited from Jessica, eliciting a rumbling purr.

I'd never had a pet growing up and was proud of how well the small creature and I had adjusted to living together. Barley was a gray and black-striped version of a wild cat minus a tail and always looked like he was having a bad hair day. The furball was also under the impression he was a dog, and I didn't have the heart to tell him otherwise.

Our daily routine began as soon as the first rays of sunlight peeked through the blinds in my bedroom. He studied me with slate-gray eyes, patiently giving me an entire minute to get out of bed before pawing my head. When that didn't work, he moved on to the other parts of my body, the ones not tucked under the comforter.

"Okay, I'm up." After pushing aside the blanket and chasing Barley off the bed, I enjoyed a leisurely stretch, then padded barefoot out of the bedroom wearing nothing but an oversized T-shirt and underwear. He'd reached the kitchen first and was pacing along the floor in front of the cabinet where I kept a plastic sealed container filled with his cat food. Gourmet salmon was his favorite, but on days when he wasn't finicky, he would gladly munch on a beefy buffet.

There was a chill in the air, and the vinyl floor was a little colder than normal. If Barley hadn't meowed as if his last meal had been weeks ago instead of the night before, I would have rushed back to my room for slippers and a housecoat.

I dumped a scoop of food in Barley's bowl, then inhaled the aroma of freshly brewed coffee, courtesy of an automatic timer I'd set the night before. I opened the cupboard to grab my favorite ceramic mug hoping it wouldn't take more than one cup of the dark roast elixir to cure my zombie-like state.

I'd barely set the cup on the counter when the air and the floor got a lot cooler.

"Ye 'ave a nice place here, Lass." The sound of a male voice jump-started my heart. A garbled shriek escaped my lips as I spun around with my arms poised, ready to execute an unpracticed version of a ninja karate chop.

Martin had made himself comfortable on my couch. He'd tucked his arms behind his head and stretched his long legs out in front of him. Fashion wasn't one of his ghostly concerns. He had on the same hat he'd been wearing the first time I met him, but it clashed with his new T-shirt and sweatpants.

"Martin, what the heck are you doing here?" I crossed my arms and glared at the booted feet resting on top of my coffee table. "You can't just pop into a person's home unannounced."

Actually, he could, but that wasn't the point. If ever there was a time I wished I'd never opened that darn box and touched the spirit seeker, it was now. Though, if I was being honest, my current predicament wasn't the magical object's fault. No, that honor rightfully belonged to Madame Minerva. She owned a magic shop in Florida and had found the seeker at a garage sale, then sold it to my father without bothering to test it first.

Martin lowered his arms and cleared his throat, seemingly bothered that I was upset with him. "Lass, I…"

I held up a hand and huffed, "My name is Rylee, remember?"

"Rylee." He acquiesced with a bow of his head.

"What I meant to say is since we are going to be seeing a lot more of each other, we need to have some ground rules," I said.

What was I thinking? He was a pirate, someone who'd spent his life on the wrong side of the law, and probably broke every rule imaginable while doing it. There was a good chance he'd ignore anything I had to say and do whatever he wanted anyway.

Instead of the annoyance I'd expected, he smirked and said, "I be listenin'."

I had a hard time believing he was going to hear anything I said, not with the way he was leering at my bare legs.

I pulled on the hem of my shirt, my growl sounding a lot like Barley's. "Stay right there." I turned and hurried along the short hallway and into the bedroom, then grabbed my housecoat off the chair sitting in the corner.

My cat was usually more fascinated with my slippers than with any of the numerous catnip-filled stuffed mice I'd purchased for him. Since one of the furry pink slip-ons was missing, I got down on my hands and knees and searched under the bed for it.

When I returned to the living room, Barley had finished eating and had jumped up on the cushioned chair in the living room to clean his paws. Martin had moved from his spot on the couch to the kitchen and was pouring a cup of coffee, which he handed to me with a smile. "Now, what are these rules ye be speakin' of?"

I took the cup, gripping the warm mug and blowing on the hot liquid. Okay, so maybe having a ghost around, especially one that could move objects, might not be so bad. It still didn't mean I would succumb to bribery easily or give him permission to pop in and out of my home whenever he wanted.

I walked over to the kitchen table, then pulled out a chair and took a seat. "First off, all rules are non-negotiable, and I can amend them as the need arises." Other than what I'd read in history books, I didn't know enough about Martin to predict what he might do. Having a family who pushed the boundaries of eccentricity taught me that having a backup plan was always best.

He leaned against the refrigerator and scowled. "Yer terms do nah seem quite fair."

I took a sip of coffee, then paused before speaking. "Yeah, well, this is my place, and I get to make the rules. Plus, I don't need you showing up at inappropriate moments."

Martin wiggled his brows. "Would the times ye be speakin' of 'ave anythin' to do with entertainin' yer new beau?"

I didn't need a mirror to know my cheeks had flushed a bright red. "What new beau?" I did a poor job of sounding like we both didn't know that he'd overheard Jade and Shawna teasing me about Logan.

"Are ye sayin' ye 'ave no interest in the detective yer friends mentioned?" Martin asked.

"My relationship with the detective is none of your business." I tamped down the urge to get even with my friends, then walked over to the table and pulled out a chair.

He snorted. "So, he has caught yer eye."

Even though Logan was a handsome guy and probably got ogled by all the single females in town, myself included, it was a topic I didn't want to discuss with Martin. Annoyed, I tapped my short fingernails on the laminated tabletop. "I was talking more about showing up in my bedroom and the bathroom... Times when I'm indisposed or not fully dressed." Thinking about Martin popping in while I was taking a shower made my cheeks heat even more.

"And just so we're clear, those two rooms are off-limits. *Forever*." It never hurt to cover any possible loopholes. I hoped my friends and I found a way to help Martin move on to his afterlife, sooner rather than later, so I wouldn't have to worry about future attempts on his part to be sneaky.

"I mean it." I shook a finger at him like my mother always did to me when she was trying to make a point.

"I be certain ye do." He flashed me a condescending grin. "I shall do me best to abide by yer wishes."

I wondered if he was this infuriating when he was alive and, if so, how many people back in his time had experienced the same urge to throttle him.

Now that we'd settled the terms of our hopefully temporary relationship, and the coffee I'd swallowed was finally kicking in, it was time to find out why Martin was here.

"Were you telling me the truth when you said you stayed behind because you didn't want to spend eternity with your crew?" I got up and stepped around him, so I could refill my mug.

He squinted. "I may 'ave exaggerated a wee bit."

The last known sighting of Martin and his crew had been nearly three hundred years ago. There'd been some speculation that his ship was lost at sea during a storm. There was a mausoleum in the local cemetery erected in his honor. I was pretty sure his body wasn't buried there, that the city founders had built it as a tourist attraction to include in the local graveyard tours.

I was curious to find out what had happened to him and what he been doing all this time. "Care to share what the wee part was and why you haven't moved on?"

"Do ye believe witches are real?" His grin faded, his tone grew somber.

"Up until this summer, I would have said no, but since you're the second spirit I've encountered, I'm trying to have an open mind." I returned to my chair and got comfortable.

"Since ye 'ave already mentioned me past occupation, then ye be aware that me crew 'n I were quite good at relievin' the wealthy of thar valuables." Martin placed his hands behind his back and paced the length of the kitchen counter. "Back in the day when I was searchin' fer treasure, I was of the same opinion. I did nah believe the rumors that a coven of the evil enchantresses lived along this coast."

I didn't know any witches. Or maybe I did. I hadn't quite decided if the Haverston sisters fell into that category yet, though I was leaning toward the yes end of the scale.

What worried me more was the curse Martin had mentioned. How long did witches live and was the one he crossed paths with still alive? And if she was, did she still live in Cumberpatch?

The subject of witches had been one of Shawna's reading favorites. When we were younger, she'd always be toting around at least one book on the topic. I was a non-believer and hadn't paid much attention when she discussed the contents with Jade and me.

"What changed your mind?" I asked.

Martin stopped to face me again. "Isabella Fernsby." He sneered, his voice oozing with disdain. "If I had heeded the warnin's about that particular wench, One-eyed Pete 'n I would nah 'ave been cursed when we tried to pilfer her family heirlooms."

"Cursed." I stammered, the hand gripping the mug shaking so badly that the coffee sloshed over the side and dripped onto the table. Learning witches existed was one thing, finding out they could actually cast a spell on someone was another.

"Aye, Lass. 'Til yesterday, I was nah able to go anywhere that me saber did nah reside."

Was it possible I'd broken his curse when I'd taken the sword from Grams? It was another item I needed to add to the growing list of questions I wanted to ask the Haverston sisters.

"Are you saying you were trapped in the blade?" I couldn't imagine what that must have been like for him, watching the world around him change and unable to be a part of it.

"Nah in it, but near it. I was able to move around, but could nah go far. Nor could anyone see me."

Even though he used words that I assumed were from his own time, he spoke with others that made him sound as if he'd been born more recently. I remembered him saying he'd watched television, and wondered if that was where he'd picked it up.

It also reminded me of his other ghostly skill, the one Jessica didn't possess. "How is it you're able to move objects?" I got up and grabbed the dishcloth draped over the sink, and cleaned up the mess I'd made.

"Spendin' time alone can be mighty borin', 'n I needed somethin' to pass the time." He smiled, then pulled out a chair and sat down next to me.

"Who is One-eyed Pete?" I asked.

His eyes sparkled at the mention of the man's name. "He be me best mate."

"If he was also cursed, then why can't I see him? Why isn't he here with you now?"

"We were each bound to a different object, a possession we were wearin' when Isabella cast her spell. Mine was me saber, 'n Pete's was his eye patch." He stared at the wall behind me as if remembering what had transpired during his encounter with the witch. "Now that I be free, I 'ave started searchin' fer 'im 'n do nah plan to leave this world 'til I find 'im."

"I guess I'm confused. What are you doing here? I mean in my apartment with me, instead of out looking for Pete?"

He sighed. "The world be a wee bit more complicated than I expected, 'n I 'ave no idea where to look. I was hopin' to gain yer help."

"If you couldn't find your friend, then how were you able to find me, to find my home?" It was a question Jessica couldn't answer because she'd been a new spirit. Since Martin had been around for a while, he might have better information.

"It ain't the same. Ye be like the beacon in a lighthouse. I can sense yer presence no matter where ye go," Martin said.

I slapped my palm on the table. "I knew it." So much for Edith and Joyce's theory that the powers of the spirit seeker would eventually wear off.

Martin wrinkled his nose. "I be sorry, wha' did ye know?"

"Nothing." I groaned and waved my hand dismissively. "It's a long story."

Freeing myself of Martin and helping him get to the spirit realm was important, but was it worth having to deal with a centuries-old witch who probably still held a grudge?

Martin must have guessed what I was thinking. "In exchange fer yer help, I shall offer me services to help ye find whoever ran that bloke through 'n spare yer uncle from bein' shackled."

I assumed his reference to shackles meant jail. I wasn't entirely sure how helpful he could be, but keeping him close might minimize the havoc he'd cause by continually popping in and out of places around town on his own. Not that me agreeing to help would keep him from doing that anyway.

No one grew up in Cumberpatch without learning all about pirate lore. None of my history lessons ever mentioned Martin or the members of his crew as being honest and trustworthy. Since Martin was partially to blame for Max's current situation, I wasn't sure if trusting him was a smart thing to do. After all, if he hadn't removed the saber from the case in the first place, then the killer would have broken the glass or found another weapon. And my uncle wouldn't be at the top of Logan's suspect list.

"Not to be skeptical or anything, but pirates don't exactly have untarnished reputations. How do I know if I agree to help you find Pete that you will keep your word?"

Martin clutched his chest. "Lass, I mean, Rylee, I be wounded by yer doubts."

Dramatic and annoying as he was, the charm he exuded was growing on me. I might regret my decision to work with him later, but for now, it seemed like the logical choice.

On the positive side, Jade and Shawna would be happy to hear I'd found out how to help him. I had a feeling searching for Martin's missing friend was going to be a lot harder than trying to find out who'd murdered Jake, especially if there were witches involved.

As much as I wanted to keep my association with the town's notorious pirate a secret, I was out of my element when it came to magical beings and curses. My friends and I were going to need help if we wanted to find Pete's eye patch.

The only person besides my father who knew more about the paranormal side of the town's history was Jade's brother Bryce. He was also the leader of the Supernatural Spoof Squashers, or spoofers, as Jade, Shawna, and I liked to call them. It wasn't much of a group. The entire membership consisted of three people: Bryce, Nate, and Myra. Maybe four since I was pretty sure my father was an honorary member.

"Fine, I'll help you find Pete."

CHAPTER FIVE

After agreeing to help Martin, he'd been more than happy to leave so I could get ready for work. Before he left, he mentioned having things he wanted to explore. I had no idea whether or not those things involved trying to find Pete or causing mischief. He also didn't specify when he planned to return. I had a feeling he'd be popping in and out the same way Jessica had.

Dealing with ghosts was not something I wanted to spend the rest of my life doing, but at the moment, it sure would be nice if I had a way to contact them instead of waiting for them to reappear randomly.

It was yet another item I needed to add to the things I planned to ask Edith and Joyce.

Since I couldn't control what Martin did, and honing babysitting skills for a ghost was not something I wanted to include on my resume, I decided it was better not knowing. Besides, helping Martin wasn't the only thing I needed to worry about. I had a shop to run, a grandmother to supervise, and an uncle's name to clear.

The great thing about having an apartment on the floor above my family's business was the ease of getting to work. I entered the building through the back entrance, then stopped in the office long enough to hang my jacket on the hook behind the door and unsnap the lead from Barley's collar. Once I set him on the floor, he rubbed against my legs, then headed for the hallway leading to the front of the shop. I turned the corner just in time to see him jump up on the checkout counter where Jade was working.

"Good morning," she said to me as she snatched Barley off the glass surface and nuzzled him against her chest.

He purred so loud even I could hear him. "Morning to you too." I glanced around the room for Grams and spotted her talking to Elliott. He was wearing his police uniform and had most likely stopped by on his way to work. I headed in their direction, hoping to find out if he had any new information on the case, but before I could ask, my grandmother beat me to it.

"I'm really sorry, Abigail, but you know I'm not allowed to discuss an ongoing case with anyone." He straightened his shoulders and jutted out his narrow, clean-shaven chin.

Grams crossed her arms and shot a scathing look at Elliott, one that had him cowering. It was no secret my grandmother could be scary when it came to protecting her family.

"Hey, Elliott." I took a step between them. "What brings you into the shop today?" Unlike my older relative, I preferred to use a subtle approach. Of course, if that didn't work, I wasn't above trying to persuade Elliott by offering him a trade of some sort.

Like my father, he had a thing for anything paranormal. When I'd needed information about Jessica's death, I'd obtained the information I needed by getting him some free tarot readings from Grams. Though I had a feeling that wasn't going to work this time, not with the way my grandmother was glaring at him.

Elliott gave me an appreciative smile. "I'm looking for

a pirate's hat and eye patch." He cleared his throat and nervously tugged on the collar of his shirt. "For my nephew's costume."

"Okay, I think you'll find what you need over here." I waited for Elliott to sidestep around Grams, then led him toward the section where we kept all the bins filled with toys and accessories for children. With the festival right around the corner, anything pirate-related received the most perusal. I'd made sure we had a wide selection and an ample supply.

He picked through several of the hats, then wrinkled his nose. "Do you have something a little bigger?"

As far as I knew, Elliott only had one nephew, and he was around eight years old. "I thought you said the hat was for your nephew?"

"Did I?" He cleared his throat. "I mean, yes, I did. He's just big for his age."

I remembered the young boy as being lanky like his uncle, only quite a bit shorter. "Okay," I tried not to sound skeptical, then aimed him toward the adult hats further down the aisle. "Maybe one of these will work better for him."

Elliott smiled, his eyes sparkling with interest. I pretended not to hear his delighted moan, then handed him a black hat with a skull and crossbones embroidered on the front. "This one is my favorite, and I'll bet the girls will love it... That is if your nephew is into girls yet."

"Drew is definitely interested." He rotated the hat in his hands, examining the front and the back.

"Why don't you try it on? You know, to see how it will look on him."

"Okay." After removing his uniform cap and tucking it under his arm, he placed the new one on his head and stepped in front of the little mirror mounted on the wall between the shelves.

Now that Elliott was relaxed and no longer worried about my grandmother, I decided it might be the only chance I got to question him about the murder. "I know Jake wasn't a very nice guy, but for someone to run him through like that..." I wrapped my arms around my waist and imitated a shudder.

"I know what you mean." He gave me a sidelong glance. "There are a couple of people I can think of that wouldn't mind seeing him gone."

"Really?" I asked, taking another hat, one with a long white feather attached to the band, off the shelf and held it out to him.

"Oh yeah, from what I hear, Jake and his partner fought all the time." After giving me the first hat, he tried on the second one, turning his head side to side and admiring the fit.

I remained silent and bobbed my head as if I'd heard the same thing. I didn't want him to realize he'd leaked important information and given me a new clue to investigate.

"I like, I mean I think Drew will like this one." He ran the feather between his thumb and forefinger.

"I'm sure you're right." I did my best to hide my amusement as I followed him to the checkout counter. I had a feeling it would be Elliott and not Drew I'd see wearing his new purchase during the festival.

It wasn't long after Elliott paid and left that the bell above the door tinkled again, and Shawna strolled inside. She'd pulled her hair back in a ponytail and was wearing her work uniform, a black skirt, and a cobalt-blue T-shirt. Stamped on the left side of her shirt was a logo bearing a pirate ship with the words "Cumberpatch Cove Cantina" printed across its center.

Normally, she worked the lunch hour and usually stopped by the shop before starting her shift. I glanced at my watch, wondering what happened to the morning, then noticed that it was only a few minutes after ten. "You're a little early today, aren't you?"

"Olivia called in sick, so Brant asked me if I could

come in and help prep for the lunch crowd."

Shawna never seemed to mind when Brant Delaney, her boss and also the restaurant's owner, called her in to work extra hours. She smiled and spread the folded newspaper out on the counter, then scooted to the side so Grams could stand next to her.

I'd expected her to follow her usual routine and jump to the page with the daily horoscope predictions. Instead, she tapped the black and white image that filled up a large portion of the *Swashbuckler Gazette's* headline page. "It looks like Jake made the news."

Leaning closer, I glimpsed the image of a sheet-covered body being wheeled away on a gurney. Somehow my friends and I had avoided getting our pictures taken by Troy, most likely because he'd been more interested in getting a photograph of the murder victim.

Town gossip traveled fast, and he had to know Jade, Shawna, and I were the ones who'd found the body. With any luck, he wouldn't bother us for a follow-up article.

Grams ran her finger along a section of the fine print. "It says here the police have a suspect in mind." She furrowed her brow. "It's a darned good thing they didn't mention Max by name. Otherwise, I'd have to go down to the newspaper office and have a talk with that young man."

I was glad Troy hadn't mentioned my uncle either. The thought of having to call my mother and tell her I'd had to bail my grandmother out of jail made me cringe.

Now that my parent's part-time retirement had transitioned into a full-time status, they had plans to travel a lot more. My father was content to see any sights my mother had on her list as long as he got to include anything paranormal in the cities they visited. My father wouldn't have agreed to see Las Vegas if there hadn't been a couple of haunted house tours close by.

"You didn't call my parents and tell them about Jake, did you?" A hint of panic laced my voice. My father already knew there was a good chance the saber belonged to Martin. The last thing I needed was for him to find out that I was being haunted by the pirate's ghost. He'd cut their vacation short and rush home for an introduction.

Besides upsetting my mother, having my father around would make any investigating I wanted to do a lot more difficult.

"No, there's nothing they can do to help right now, and I don't want to ruin their vacation. Which reminds me." Grams narrowed her gaze, scrutinizing each of us in turn, saving me for last. "What were you three doing on Max's boat yesterday?"

My friends and I had a long-standing rule that we didn't share our exploits with anyone else without discussing it amongst ourselves first. Family members were at the top of the list. Since we'd already made a pact regarding my ghostly gift when we were helping Jessica, the rules still applied.

Jade and Shawna gave me a supportive look to let me know they wouldn't say anything without my permission, not that it mattered. My grandmother had a way of finding things out all on her own.

Luckily, the bell above the door jingled, announcing a customer's arrival. Grams scowled, letting me know the interruption was only a temporary postponement. With a cheery good morning, she circled the counter and offered the newcomers her assistance.

"Did you tell her about you know who?" Jade asked as soon as Grams was out of hearing distance.

"Not yet." I knew I'd have to tell her eventually, but I wanted to discuss what I'd learned from Martin with my friends first.

"Speaking of the forbidden topic, have you talked to him since yesterday?" Shawna opened the newspaper to the page containing daily horoscopes, then refolded it before placing it back on the counter.

I shifted sideways so I could keep an eye on my

grandmother. "He popped into my apartment this morning."

Jade raised her brow with a grin. "How did that go?"

"After I got over being scared half to death, not bad," I said. "Though I did point out that he needed to stay out of my bedroom and bathroom."

Jade giggled. "I'm surprised you didn't tell him your entire apartment was off-limits."

I snorted. "I probably should have, but I got the impression he'd just ignore me."

"Did you get a chance to find out why he's still here and what we need to do to help him?" Shawna asked as she continued to peruse the paper.

"I did." I leaned a little closer to my friends and kept my voice lowered. "Remember the discussions we had in history class, the ones about whether or not Martin and his crew had encountered a storm and their ship had disappeared at sea?"

"Yeah." Shawna finally gave us her full attention.

"Well, the sinking boat part might be correct, but Martin wasn't on board because he'd been cursed by a witch." I quickly shared the details Martin had given me, including his refusal to move on until he found Pete.

"Whoa, that's huge. Does it mean you're cursed now too because you touched his saber?" Shawna glanced at my hands as if she expected to see something ominous.

Up until now, the thought hadn't occurred to me.

Jade frowned at Shawna. "Don't you think she'd know if she was cursed?"

"Who's cursed?" Hearing Grams had all of us jumping. We'd been too involved in our conversation to notice that she'd finished helping her customer.

"Rylee," Shawna blurted.

I shook my head and groaned. My friend never could withstand any of my grandmother's interrogations.

"What do you mean she's cursed?" She placed her hands on her hips, her eyes widening with understanding.

"Does this have anything to do with that shock you received from the saber?"

My grandmother should have been a detective; her sleuthing skills rivaled Logan's.

"Yeah." The line between outright fibbing and not sharing information was slim. Now that Shawna had blabbed, there was no point trying to keep Martin's haunting a secret from her any longer. I spent the next five minutes catching her up on my meeting with Martin and my newest endeavor to help him reach the spirit realm.

"So Max was right, the saber really does belong to Martin," Grams said.

"Uh-huh," Shawna said. "It also explains how it ended up outside the case, but not how Jake ended up skewed with it."

"So, our goal is to find this Pete person, correct?" It sounded like Grams was offering her help, whether I wanted it or not.

"Hopefully, all we have to do is find the eye patch," I said.

"So you can free Pete's spirit by touching it like you did the saber," Jade said as she walked to a nearby shelf and replaced the bottle of herbs Barley had knocked on the floor.

I wasn't looking forward to being zapped again, but if it meant being ghost-free, I'd gladly do it.

***

For the next few hours, the shop saw a steady flow of customers. The most recent was a woman with her two daughters. The little girls appeared to be close in age, probably somewhere in the seven to nine-year-old vicinity. They'd stubbornly refused to leave until their mother bought them each their own plastic sword.

Anyone who grew up in our town and attended as many pirate festivals as my friends and I did, had acquired swashbuckling skills. The purchase had quickly turned into a dueling match that included a few pointers from Jade and me.

By the time they'd worn themselves out and were leaving, Max was arriving. The smaller of the two girls tipped her head back to look up at my uncle, then pulled on her sister's sleeve. "Do you think he's a real pirate?"

"I am," Max said with a wink. "I even have my own boat and go on treasure hunts almost every day." Always the salesman, he fished a business card out of his vest pocket and handed it to their mother. By the way the woman was grinning at him as she ushered the girls out the door, I had no doubt she'd be taking her daughters on one of his tours.

"Maxwell." Grams pulled him into a hug as if it had been years since she'd seen him and not a couple of days. "Are you all right?"

"I'm fine." He returned her hug, rolling his hazel eyes at me and gaining and awe from Jade.

"I'm surprised to see you dressed for work." She took a step back. "I thought your boat was considered a crime scene."

"Technically, they couldn't find any evidence to prove the murder happened on the *Delight*, so Roy gave me permission to resume business."

From what I'd gathered, Logan and his uncle didn't always agree on law enforcement procedures. I wondered if he'd approved of Roy's decision.

"What brings you by the shop?" Grams said over her shoulder as she led him to the area where Jade and I were standing. "You didn't already use up the supplies we delivered, did you?"

"No, it's nothing like that." Max tugged on his beard. "Lucas called in sick and made it sound as if he wasn't going to be able to work tomorrow, either."

"Shawna said Olivia was sick as well. Do you think something is going around?" Grams glanced at the herbal aisle, probably contemplating which preventative concoction she should be taking.

"Not that I'm aware of," Max said.

Before we all ended up the victims of a healthy regimen, I changed the subject. "Your reason for being here was…"

My uncle knew what I was doing and grinned. "With Lucas being out, I'm a little shorthanded and haven't been able to find anyone to cover his shift. I heard Josh was in town, and I was going to stop by Mattie's to see if he'd be willing to fill in for a couple of days."

Mattie was my grandmother's best friend and owned the coffee shop across the street. Her nephew Josh never missed a pirate festival, so I wasn't surprised to hear that he was visiting. Like my friends and I, he'd spent a couple of summers working for my uncle and wouldn't need any additional training to help him with the tours.

Thinking about tours reminded me of what Elliott had said about the arguments Jake had with his partner. The sales office for the Sea Witch Pirate Tours was located on the same block as Max's business. "If it's okay with Grams, I can help out tomorrow."

I figured volunteering would give me the perfect opportunity to get more information about my only clue. Being away from the shop would make more work for Grams and Jade, so I gave my grandmother an imploring look hoping she'd wait until Max left before asking me to explain.

Jade interceded by flashing me a sly grin and said, "I think that's a great idea." She tucked her arm through Grams. "We should be able to spare Rylee for a couple of days, don't you think?"

Grams tsked. "Would it matter if I said no?"

I draped my arm across her shoulders and leaned my head against hers. "Probably not."

"Wonderful." Max clapped his hands together. "Why don't you come by a little early in the morning and I'll have

Chloe show you what she needs help with." He was halfway to the door when he turned and said, "Don't forget to wear your old uniform."

"I won't." My smile faded. The outfit hadn't left the back of my closet in years. I was certain I'd put on a few pounds since the last time I'd worn it and had no idea whether or not it would still fit. It would probably be okay since I'd only be helping for one or two days and I didn't think my uncle would mind what I wore as long as I looked like a pirate.

The bell tinkled just as Max reached for the door handle. He immediately took a step back, giving Amanda Dankworth a wide berth as she entered the shop carrying a large plastic clothes bag draped over her arm.

"Max," she acknowledged him through gritted teeth. Her sneer enhanced by the red spreading across her high-boned cheeks.

"Amanda," he replied with an equally sarcastic tone.

Max and Amanda had dated for the longest time, and I'd thought for sure they'd get married. For whatever reason, their relationship hadn't ended well, and the two of them spent the last few years doing their best to avoid each other. Not an easy task in a town where most of the residents knew each other. A situation made worse whenever Cumberpatch celebrated one of its many festivities, and a lot of the shop owners and businesses participated.

As soon as Amanda stepped inside, Max couldn't move fast enough to slip around her and leave the shop.

After shooting another disdainful glare through the glass door, Amanda turned, a forced smile on her face. Even though things between her and my uncle seemed strained, she never let it interfere with the way she treated the other members of our family.

"Good morning, Abigail." She patted the plastic bag as she headed in our direction. "I finished the modifications you requested for your costume."

Amanda was an awesome seamstress and owned the Barbary Boutique, the only costume shop in town. The perfectly tailored gray slacks and pastel pink shirt she wore were a perfect example of her handiwork. She also did logo embroidery and supplied uniforms for most of the local businesses.

"Hi, Rylee, Jade." Amanda's voice held a hint of surprise as if she hadn't noticed us when she'd first entered the shop. "Are you doing all right? I heard you're the ones who found Jake."

I'd thought it was odd that she was making a personal delivery when she normally sent a text or called when an order was ready. After hearing Jake's name, I wondered if she'd heard the murder weapon belonged to Max and was hoping we'd give her some juicy details about what we saw.

I didn't think Amanda's question about our welfare had anything to do with lingering feelings she might have for my uncle. She was a notorious gossiper, and I was afraid she'd be vindictive enough to spread rumors about him. Since Max was already on Logan's suspect list, I didn't want to make things worse by giving her information that was none of her business. Information she'd no doubt embellish.

Amanda didn't give Jade and me a chance to answer. "I can't say I'm surprised about what happened to him." She draped the bag across the glass counter near the cash register, then began unzipping it. "He wasn't a very nice man."

"No, he wasn't." Grams moved closer to see the bag's contents.

Amanda released a heavy sigh. "And everyone knows he and Max didn't get along."

I'd bet a week's worth of chocolate if Amanda came across anyone who didn't know, she'd make it a point to provide them with details.

"So, what happened when you talked to the police? I

heard they had that yellow tape up everywhere and were questioning everyone who happened to be on the docks." Amanda waved her hand dramatically through the air. "I also heard that Roy's nephew moved to town and will be working on the case."

"Detective Prescott is good at his job, and I'm sure he'll find the *real* killer." I'd had enough of Amanda's insinuations about my uncle, not to mention her rambling was getting on my nerves. "I've got some work to do in the back. Holler if you need me, Grams." I glimpsed Jade's please-take-me-with-you look before I escaped down the hallway.

I felt bad about leaving Jade behind and promised myself that I'd make it up to her later. Right now, I needed some alone time to figure out my game plan for tomorrow.

CHAPTER SIX

Surprisingly, the uniform I used to wear when I worked for my uncle still fit. The velvety burgundy skirt was a little tight around the waist, but I had no problem getting it zipped. The top was a short-sleeved off-white blouse with a one-inch ruffle running along the entire neckline. A wide black leather belt that laced in the front, along with a pair of thigh-high boots, completed the outfit. I even found a black scarf, which I draped across the top of my head and knotted at my nape.

There wasn't any parking allowed by the shops in the area near the dock, so I left my car in one of the visitor lots and walked several blocks to reach my uncle's business. People, mostly tourists, strolled along the sidewalks, occasionally slowing to view the displays in the souvenir shops. Others stopped to admire the waterfront view and take pictures.

Chloe had already arrived and was unlocking the front door to the ticket office by the time I got there. Her pirate attire was similar to what she'd been wearing the last time Jade, Shawna, and I saw her.

"Hey, Rylee." Her smile seemed more practiced than genuine as if I'd interrupted her thoughts. "Max told me you were coming, and I'm happy for the help."

"Not a problem." The tension I'd sensed continued after following her inside. "It's been a while since I've worked here, so I hope you don't mind giving me a refresher." Just in case her anxiety stemmed from having to work with the boss's niece, I wanted to reassure her that I was only here to help not take over her job. It would also make finding out anything she knew about what happened to Jake a lot easier.

I didn't know for sure when Jake had met his demise. Asking Logan for the information, even in an innocent manner, would only earn me another lecture, so I squelched the idea. Most of the businesses along the docks, my uncle's shop included, didn't open until ten. Since I'd seen Jake late in the afternoon the day before my friends and I found him, I assumed his encounter with the saber had happened sometime during the night or possibly in the early morning hours.

I listened while Chloe explained how to use the cash register and the process they used for issuing tour tickets, which hadn't changed much based on what I remembered.

I'd been contemplating the best way to ask Chloe questions about Jake when she said, "Just so you know, we've been busier than usual ever since the police pulled Jake out of the water." She grabbed a stack of brochures off the shelf beneath the counter and set them next to the register. "A lot of people who stop by have been asking questions about the murder." Her matter-of-fact tone suggested she wasn't bothered by it.

"Good to know." I picked up one of the pamphlets and opened it, pretending to be interested in the information posted inside. "Just curious, what have you been telling them?"

Her shoulders tensed. "There's not much I can say. I didn't see anything, at least not until after…"

"My friends and I found him." I finished for her.

"Yeah." She twisted the silver ring she wore on the

pinky finger of her right hand. "That must have been horrible."

"It wasn't too bad, but it's also not something I'd wish on others." It would probably take months before the image of Jake bobbing in the water faded from my mind, if ever.

Even though Chloe said she hadn't seen anything, it was possible she might know something. With the Sea Witch's office so close, and the walkway out front the only way to access their boat, she must have seen Jake and his crew pass by regularly. "Can you think of anybody who might have wanted to get rid of Jake?"

She released a nervous laugh. "It's a pretty long list...although, now that you ask, I did see Jake arguing with Lucas last week."

"Do you have any idea what they were arguing about?" When Chloe headed outside to set the folding wooden sign listing the various tour prices on the sidewalk, I trailed after her.

"No, but Lucas seemed angry. When he shoved Jake, I thought for sure they were going to get into a fistfight."

"But they didn't?" I asked, following her back inside.

Chloe shook her head. "Lucas stormed away and refused to say anything when I asked him about it later."

I wasn't an expert, and I didn't think getting into a heated argument was a good enough reason to commit murder. Until the police found the killer, I assumed everyone who'd tangled with Jake was a possible suspect.

If my theory about someone trying to make Max look guilty was correct, then what was Lucas's motivation? Was the fight he had with Jake somehow connected to my uncle? So far, Lucas's argument was the only clue I'd been able to uncover. It might be nothing, but I still wanted to follow up on it. Since he was out sick and wouldn't be coming to work for at least one more day, any plans to question him would have to wait.

"Good morning, ladies." Max appeared in the doorway.

He wore one of his many pirate outfits, a benefit from dating Amanda, and had a backpack slung across his shoulder.

"Morning," Chloe and I replied at the same time.

"Rylee, will you be okay by yourself if Chloe helps me on the first tour?" he asked.

I leaned against the counter. "I should be able to handle it without any problems." I was glad I'd be working alone. It would give me a chance to check out the neighboring businesses without having to explain what I was doing to Chloe. It would also make things easier should Martin decide to make an appearance.

I hadn't seen him after our discussion in my apartment. Maybe he'd found Pete on his own and wouldn't need my help after all.

"Great, we should be back in a few hours." Max stepped aside to make room for Chloe to leave ahead of him.

No sooner had they disappeared from view, then people started showing up to buy tickets. The next thirty minutes was a frenzy of answering questions and handling purchases.

"Enjoy the tour." I handed the last man in line a ticket along with a brochure. When I reached for more pamphlets to replenish the stack on the counter, a ripple of cold air skimmed across my skin.

"Did ye miss me, Lass?" Martin appeared a lot closer to me than I'd expected, then chuckled when I gasped, and the folded papers I was clutching flew through the air.

He'd secured his dark brown hair at his nape and dressed like a tourist again. Only today, he was wearing a T-shirt with a floral button-down shirt done in bright blues and reds, and a pair of lace-up sneakers instead of his boots.

"No," I drew the word out with a frown.

"Nah even a wee bit?" He pouted, then hopped up to sit on the counter with his legs hanging over the edge.

As incorrigible as he was, I had a hard time staying irritated with him. "Where have you been?" *And should I be worried?* I knelt to pick up the brochures I'd dropped. After shoveling them into a neat pile, I placed them on the counter a few feet away from him.

"Out having a wee bit of fun." He winked, his wide grin making me nervous.

I'd already witnessed his idea of having fun with water cannons and hoped he hadn't done something worse. I decided it might not be a bad idea to check the *Gazette* later to see if anyone had reported any unusual and hard to explain occurrences.

I had enough going on, and the last thing I needed was a prankster ghost. "I hope you're doing your best to be inconspicuous while you're having your wee bit of fun."

His snort confirmed my suspicions and concerned me even more.

"Wha' be the game we be playin' today?" Martin asked.

It took me a second to figure out what he meant. "Are you asking me about the game plan?"

"Aye." He wrapped his arms across his chest. "I assume ye 'ave put yer resourcefulness to good use 'n come up with a way to find Pete."

"I have one or two ideas," I said, not feeling as confident about my abilities as he seemed to be.

"Good, then let us be off." He hopped off the counter and circled behind me.

"Wait, I can't just leave, I have work to do."

Footsteps filtered in from outside. "Wait, this is the one, I know it." Martin and I both froze the instant the woman who was speaking moved into the open doorway. Her facial features, dark eyes, and square jaw seemed vaguely familiar. I didn't realize why until Lavender Abbott appeared next to her.

Dread skittered along my spine, and I bit back a groan. After everything I'd been through this week, seeing the woman who'd gone out of her way to make my life difficult ever since high school pretty much guaranteed the rest of my day wasn't going to go well. I'd never figured out the truth behind her dislike for my family. It had something to do with our grandmothers, supposedly a secret that no one was willing to talk about.

"I don't care, Trudy. Let's go." Lavender pursed her lips and disdainfully glanced around the inside of the shop.

I'd only met her cousin a couple of times, and the last I'd heard, she'd gotten married and lived somewhere in the Midwest.

Trudy ignored Lavender, then adjusted the large pink shopping bag hanging on her arm as she took a few more steps. "You have the boat where they found the dead guy, right?"

I gripped the edge of the counter, wishing it wasn't too late to lock the door and pretend the shop was closed. "Actually, the body was found in the water, *not* on the boat."

"And you would know that wouldn't you, Rylee, since I heard you're the one who found him." Lavender sneered.

Recognition flared in Trudy's dark eyes, her smile fading. "Rylee as in Spencer. I thought you looked familiar."

The Abbotts had perfected the use of condescending tones, and I'd perfected the skill of ignoring them. Martin, on the other hand, seemed to take offense and leveled a scathing glare at both women.

Up until now, he'd been a good little ghost, standing off to the side with his hands tucked in his pockets. "Are these wenches friends of yers?"

Unless my cell phone magically rang on its own, I couldn't use it as a prop to speak with him. I tapped the counter with my fingertips, drawing Trudy and Lavender's attention long enough to give my head a subtle shake.

"She's the one who found Jessica too," Lavender said to Trudy. "Seems like quite a coincidence that she's always around whenever someone ends up dead."

Although I hadn't been anywhere near Jessica's body when she'd been found, reminding Lavender of the fact would be moot.

Before my friend's murder, Lavender had voiced her disappointment on numerous occasions about being replaced by Jessica as the lead for the Founders Day treasure hunt. At one point, shortly after my friends and I found a doubloon in the Abbott crypt, we'd added Lavender and her sister Serena to our list of suspects.

I could feel the heat rising on my cheeks. My parents had always stressed the need for acting professional whenever we were in the shop and dealing with difficult customers. Since my parents weren't around, and they'd never said anything about my behavior applying to my uncle's business, I'd decided the rules didn't apply.

"Funny, I…"

Martin didn't give me a chance to finish my retort. He walked over to Trudy, yanked the bag from her arm, then waved it around several times before slowly setting it on the floor near her feet.

To me, Martin's performance didn't look strange, to anyone who couldn't see him, it appeared as if the bag was levitating on its own.

Trudy's face paled, and she shook her finger at Lavender. "You, you…never told me she was a witch." She stumbled backward, then scrambled from view the second she reached the sidewalk.

Lavender stared at me as if she'd just had a lifetime suspicion confirmed. "I don't know how you did that,"— she grabbed the bag off the floor—"but I intend to find out." With a spin that caused the bag to bounce off the door frame, she hollered Trudy's name and stomped out of the building.

Anger replaced my disbelief. Lavender had been an annoyance for years, but Martin's little trick had given her the fuel she needed to become a major pain in my backside. "That's just great," I snapped, throwing my hands in the air and glaring at Martin. "Now, thanks to you, everyone in town is going to think I'm a supernatural being who can perform magic."

"Ye can speak to ghosts." He smiled smugly. "Does that nah qualify as magical?"

"Right now, it qualifies as being cursed…by you." Somewhere in the back of my mind, I'd reasoned that if Martin could move objects, then tossing one at him wouldn't go through him. Maybe smacking him in the head, even if he were dead and couldn't feel pain, would knock some sense into him, make him think about the ramifications of his pranks before he acted on them.

At the very least, it would make me feel better. I picked up a souvenir coffee mug off the display shelf mounted on a nearby wall. I would gladly pay eight dollars to test my theory.

Martin stared at my weapon, his eyes widening. "Rylee," he cautioned, then disappeared when I raised my arm, threatening to throw it. Even though I was going to regret what he'd done later, I couldn't help smiling when I remembered the shocked look on Lavender's and Trudy's faces.

If nothing else, I'd gotten him to use my name. After returning the cup to the shelf, I inhaled several deep breaths, which did nothing to relieve my frustration. I was determined, more now than ever, to find Pete and hurry their trip to the afterlife.

***

By the time Max and Chloe had returned, and I'd joined my friends for our prearranged lunch, my irritation with Martin had subsided, but not by much.

Ye Olde Angler had the best fish and chips in town and was one of the most popular food places located near the pier. I walked underneath the hand-carved wooden sign with the restaurant's name and a large fish about to swallow a hook, then turned the corner of the building leading to their outside patio.

Luckily, Shawna and Jade had arrived early enough to snag a large table in the corner, complete with an overhead umbrella. They'd also placed our order, the waitress delivering the food when I'd arrived.

My friends were wearing brightly colored outfits and looked as if they'd stepped out of a crayon box. Shawna's blue shirt matched the streaks in her hair, and Jade wore a teal dress enhanced with a shiny black belt.

Since neither of them had mentioned Nate would be joining us, I was a little surprised to see him sitting next to Shawna with his arm draped across the back of her chair. If they were officially dating, it was possible she'd forgotten to mention it.

"I got you your favorite." Shawna pointed at the platter containing a cod sampler special sitting on the table next to a vacant seat.

"She even got you extra French fries." Jade unfolded a paper napkin, then placed it on her lap.

Since this lunch was supposed to be the three of us, the extra food was Shawna's way of apologizing for dragging Nate along. It didn't bother me near as much as it would have if the rest of the spoofers had shown up.

My stomach rumbled as I took a seat. "Thanks." I snatched one of the curly potatoes with special seasoning off my plate and took a bite. If Nate hadn't been sitting with us, I would have moaned my appreciation for the delectable morsel.

After a few minutes where the only noise was the sound of food being consumed, Nate asked, "So how's the sleuthing going?"

I was pretty sure Shawna was the one who'd blabbed, and I reconsidered whether or not the additional food was a good enough bribe.

"What?" She waved a fry in Jade's face after being nudged with her elbow. "I didn't say anything. He figured it out all by himself."

"Shawna's right." Nate pushed his long bangs off his forehead. "All she did was tell me your uncle owned the saber used to kill Jake, and I assumed you guys would try to find out who did it… Like you did the last time."

Since he hadn't mentioned Martin's ghost, I was confident he didn't know, and I wouldn't have to hurt my friend for sharing secrets.

"The sleuthing isn't going as well as I'd hoped." The one clue I'd gotten from Chloe about Lucas still seemed lame, so I decided to wait and share it with my friends later.

Shawna dipped a piece of fish in her tartar sauce. "You know how the experts are always saying a criminal returns to the scene of a crime?"

"Yes, why?" Jade asked.

"Maybe the murderer showed up after the police arrived," Shawna said.

Nate snapped his fingers. "That's entirely possible." He glanced at the three of us in turn. "Can any of you remember who was standing in the crowd on the dock?"

"I noticed a couple of shop owners, but I think most of the people hanging around were curious tourists." Jade reached for her drink, then stopped before taking a sip. "Oh, and I remember seeing Chloe and Lucas, but they were working in the tour shack and probably came outside when they heard the commotion."

"What about the day Max and Jake had their argument?" Shawna glanced at me. "Can you remember who was there?"

"Not really." I'd been too busy trying to stop Martin after he'd doused everybody. "It was mostly tourists that day too. Grams was leaving for her appointment with Nadine, and she might have seen something." I picked up another fry. "Though I doubt it."

I'd just finished swallowing and was reaching for my soda when the chair next to me moved by itself. A few seconds later, Martin appeared in the seat.

Other than open-mouthed stares, I had to give Shawna and Jade credit for not reacting. Nate, not so much. He jumped to his feet and was backing away from the table. "I, I... Jessica's not back, is she?"

I grabbed the back of the chair, pretending I was the one who had moved it as I glanced around to see if anyone sitting at the nearby tables had noticed.

Shawna shot Nate a disbelieving glare. "No, it's not Jessica." She looked as if she wanted to wrestle him to the ground when she grabbed his sleeve and tugged him back towards his seat. I had a feeling the mention of Nate's ex might put a damper on their future dating. The shoulder shrug and knowing glance Jade gave me said she was thinking the same thing.

Cheeks flushed, Nate sat back down and did his best not to stare at the empty seat, which was a little hard when Martin scooted the chair closer to the table.

"What part of inconspicuous don't you understand?" I whispered sarcastically at Martin, my irritation with him renewed.

"Me apologies, Lass." Martin grinned, then propped his elbows on the tabletop. "Will the lad,"—he tipped his head toward Nate—"also be helpin' with our quest?"

I gritted my teeth and glared in Nate's direction. "Not if he doesn't stop staring."

"Oh, yeah, right." Though Nate focused his attention on his empty plate, he continued to shoot curious glances towards the empty chair. "Are you going to tell me who's, you know...visiting?"

Now that Nate knew we weren't alone, there was no reason not to tell him who it was. Sharing with Nate also meant Bryce and Myra would find out a lot sooner than I'd hoped.

After receiving a reluctant, yet approving nod from me, Shawna leaned closer to Nate and whispered, "It's Martin Cumberpatch."

"No way, that's so…"

Jade interrupted by clearing her throat. "Not to change the subject, but is anyone surprised that Jake's death hasn't slowed down business for the Sea Witch's tours?" She directed her gaze to the shop on the opposite side of the street.

She was the best when it came to keeping us all on track, and had even perked Martin's interest. I shifted slightly to get a better look at the building housing my uncle's competition. Arlene, the supposedly grieving widow, had arrived. She was standing outside, her face beaming as she spoke to Braden. With Jake gone, did it mean the two of them were now business partners?

"Arlene doesn't seem too broken up about losing her husband, either." Jade wrinkled her pert nose. "He's only been dead a couple of days, and she's not even wearing black."

Jade constantly tried to improve my wardrobe, and I should have known she'd noticed anything out of place when it came to fashion. Even I had to agree that the tight-fitting red dress with matching heels seemed a little too much for the new widow. Though, judging by the once over glance Braden had given her, I was pretty sure he disagreed.

Shawna took the last fry off her plate and wiggled it in the air. "You know, it's a known fact that most murders are committed by the spouse or a close member of the family."

"I've heard that too." Nate agreed a little too enthusiastically, possibly trying to make amends to Shawna for bringing up Jessica.

It seemed to work because Shawna smiled. "Notice Arlene's body language, the way she's leaning closer to Braden and attentively listens to what he says."

"Yeah," Nate said, paying closer attention to the couple.

Arlene's overdramatic display was enough to make me

nauseous. It was even worse than the tantrum she'd thrown the day she'd blamed Max for Jake's murder.

Shawna pushed her plate aside. "How much do you want to bet those two are doing it, and probably conspired to get rid of Jake?"

"What be they doin'?" Martin furrowed his brow, his glance jumping from my friend to me.

I coughed, nearly choking on the piece of fish I'd swallowed. I wasn't about to explain the intricacies of modern-day interactions between men and women with a centuries-old ghost in front of my friends. "We'll talk about it later." It was a conversation I didn't want to have in private either and hoped he'd forget about it. Or better yet, I'd make Shawna tell him since she was the one who'd brought it up in the first place.

I glanced at the watch on my wrist, noting the time and glad I could use it to change the direction of the conversation before Shawna blurted out something even more embarrassing. "I should probably get going."

"What about discussing the plan to help our mutual friend?" Shawna gazed in Martin's direction.

"It will have to wait. I need to cover so Chloe can help Max with his next tour."

Nate's disappointed sigh was louder than Shawna's. I'd assumed Martin's silence while he watched Braden and Arlene was due to disappointment or his lack of anything to add to the current conversation.

"I believe I understand Shawna's reference to doin' it." A mischievous glint flickered in his eyes and his grin widened. "Perhaps the scoundrel requires a lesson about chivalry 'n abstinence when it comes to another man's wench."

I was glad to hear that Martin's pirating past left him with a few morals. Although I wasn't happy when he disappeared without moving his chair and reappeared next to Arlene. Yelling at him to stop whatever he was thinking about doing would only draw Arlene and Braden's attention to my friends and me. The last thing I needed after the Trudy episode was to be anywhere near what appeared to be a magical event to anyone who couldn't see Martin.

The couple sitting at the table next to us got up to leave, the man taking the Styrofoam cup containing his drink with him. They continued their conversation as they strolled away from us and toward the spot where Martin was standing. The second the man walked past Arlene, Martin grabbed the drink out of his hand and poured it along the front of Braden's pants.

"No, no, no," I muttered, then gripped the edge of the table when Braden and the unsuspecting guy shared some heated words. Obviously proud of the chaos he'd caused, Martin chuckled, then with a wink and another one of his exaggerated bows, he had the audacity to disappear.

I wasn't one for swearing, but I was tempted to start. Martin had to be the most exasperating ghost I'd ever met, not that I'd met many. It was a darned good thing he was already dead; otherwise, I'd be willing to dig a grave for him myself.

"Maybe we should do something to help." Nate scooted his chair away from the table.

I glanced at Shawna and Jade who looked equally concerned and prepared to intercede if necessary. Chances are anything we did would make things worse. We couldn't tell the two men that a ghost was responsible for spilling the drink out of a misguided chivalrous notion. Though I doubted being honorable was Martin's real motivation.

Even though I wasn't to blame, I still felt responsible and turned to get out of my seat. "I'll take care of it."

"Rylee, wait." Shawna jutted her chin. "It looks like it's under control."

Whatever Arlene said before dragging Braden inside the building had ended the exchange. Relieved that no one had gotten hurt, I removed my death grip on the table. "Martin's gone, so now might be a good time to leave."

With a silent consensus, everyone got out of their chairs and moved and headed for the main sidewalk.

While Shawna and Nate headed toward the lot where they'd parked, Jade pulled me aside and said, "I didn't want to say anything in front of Nate, but you know who we should be asking for help, right?"

"I do." I hated to admit she might be right. I hadn't wanted to involve any more people, but if anyone could find out more information about the jeweled eye patch belonging to Pete, it would be her brother Bryce. "Let me think about it, and I'll get back to you.

CHAPTER SEVEN

I didn't mind working for my uncle, but one day turned into two, and I was glad when Max phoned to tell me Lucas was returning, and he no longer needed my help. According to Grams, with the festival only a couple of days away, things at the shop had been busy but manageable.

Even though I'd arrived early, I hadn't been much help because it was mid-afternoon by the time I finished catching up on the pile of paperwork stacked on my desk. I'd heard the bell above the door jingle numerous times and knew if things got crazy, Grams and Jade would let me know.

After placing several files in the lateral cabinet sitting next to the wall opposite my desk, I headed for the front of the building. I'd barely reached the checkout counter when I heard a murpy meow, which sounded more like a shrill battle cry. Seconds later, a flash of fur filled my peripheral, and Barley landed on the display case next to me.

He'd launched himself from a shelf on the wall. The ledge was so high and out of the way that I needed a tall ladder to reach it. Since I'd never actually witnessed him making the ascent, I couldn't figure out how he continued to get up there.

He strutted toward me, wearing a burgundy vest and a cat-sized hat embroidered with a white skull and crossbones in the center of the black fabric. While I'd been away from the shop, my friends had turned my beloved pet into a miniature pirate. Even worse, Barley didn't seem to mind. "Whose idea was it to dress Barley in a costume?" My inquisitive gaze jumped from Jade to Grams.

"Shawna ordered the outfit for him." Jade walked up and scratched him behind the ears. "Cute, right?"

"Oh, yeah…adorable," I groaned. The holiday season would be starting in a couple of months, and I dreaded to see what Shawna had planned for the furry creature during Halloween. Though I should be thankful my friend hadn't decided to dye his fur with blue streaks to match hers. I didn't voice my fear out loud just in case Jade jokingly mentioned it to Shawna.

Jade picked up Barley and set him on the floor. "Now that Nate knows about Martin, it's only a matter of time before he tells Bryce if he hasn't already. Have you given my suggestion about asking him for his help any thought?"

"I have, but I want to visit the Booty Bizarre first to see if they have the eye patch before we involve the spoofers." I wasn't looking forward to dealing with Myra. She'd been extremely skeptical when she heard I could see Jessica's ghost. I could only imagine what her reaction was going to be once I told her about Martin.

I'd been so preoccupied with my ponderings that I hadn't heard the bell or noticed our newest visitor until Grams spoke a little louder than normal. "Good afternoon, Detective. What can we do for you?"

My grandmother's tone was sweeter than usual. Her being overly nice to the man who suspected her son of murder made me wary.

"I was hoping to speak with Rylee." He glanced around the room until he spotted me.

I associated the intense gaze that held mine with his detective mode and assumed he hadn't stopped by to say hello. The excited flutter I felt when he'd first entered the shop quickly turned into an uncomfortable knot. "Is this visit personal or business-related?" I asked, hoping it wasn't the latter.

The ends of his lips lifted into an amused grin. "A little of both, but mostly business."

Even though I was disappointed, I had to give the guy points for being honest.

"Do you have time to get a coffee?" Logan asked.

"Of course she does," Grams said.

"Go." Jade smiled, then gave me a gentle nudge in Logan's direction. "We can manage without you for a while."

I glared at both women, letting them know I was quite capable of answering for myself. They could have saved their meddling. If Logan was here to discuss my uncle, it was a conversation I looked forward to having.

"I guess so," I said, then followed him outside. When it looked as if he planned to go across the street to Mattie's Coffee Shop, I took his hand and pulled him to the right. "I know a better place if you're looking for a little privacy."

Mattie's place had the best coffee and served a wide selection of tasty home-baked goodies, including my favorite cream cheese muffins.

If it wasn't for my grandmother's penchant for getting into trouble and always conspiring to find me a boyfriend, I wouldn't have passed up the opportunity to visit the shop. The last thing I needed was her best friend Mattie spying on Logan and me, then reporting what she'd seen or overheard back to Grams.

Logan didn't argue, nor did he release my hand until he stopped to open the door to the ice cream shop a block away. They didn't do the same amount of business that Mattie's place did, so there was hardly anyone waiting in line.

"Two coffees," he said to the teenage girl working behind the counter. She'd been dreamily eyeing him since we'd walked inside. Not that I could blame her, I'd been guilty of doing the same thing myself.

"Do you need any cream or sugar to go with these?" she asked as she sat two Styrofoam cups on the counter.

Logan gave me a questioning glance, which I answered with a shake of my head.

"Black is fine, thanks." After paying for the drinks, he urged me toward an empty table in the corner away from any other customers.

I hadn't seen Martin since he disappeared after dousing Braden. Hopefully, I'd get lucky, and he wouldn't make one of his surprise appearances and intrude, then complicate my time with Logan.

After taking a sip of his drink, Logan studied me as if deciding the best way to start a conversation. "I understand the day before you found Jake that he was arguing with your uncle on the dock near his ship."

I was well aware of his interrogating techniques and wasn't going to offer any information until I found out what he already knew and what he was after. I blew on my coffee, holding his gaze, and waiting for him to continue. It didn't take long for him to realize he wasn't going to get anywhere without sharing first.

With a sigh, he shook his head and said, "Rylee."

"Hmm."

"I know you were there that day."

"Fine." I set my cup back on the table, then wrapped my fingers around the base.

Logan and I hadn't known each other long, but I'd gotten good at reading his body language. When he raised an inquiring brow, I knew we weren't leaving until he got an answer.

"Truthfully, I didn't see much. One of the water cannons was malfunctioning, people were getting drenched, and I was too busy trying to fix the problem."

Unless Logan asked me specifics about the malfunction, which happened to be Martin, he was getting a reasonably accurate accounting of the truth.

"The boat was right next to the dock. Are you sure you didn't hear anything that might be helpful?" Logan asked.

"I'm pretty sure." I couldn't tell him I'd been too shocked from seeing our town's notorious pirate to pay much attention to anything else. "I don't want to tell you how to run your investigation, but maybe you should be questioning the people who were standing on the dock and actually saw something."

Rather than take offense, he gave me one of those grins that always made me melt inside. "I already have."

More curious than wary, I asked, "If you already have the information, then why are you questioning me?"

"Because I wanted to spend some time with you, and this way, I knew you wouldn't say no." He took another swallow of his drink.

I couldn't help being charmed by his candor, nor could I stop myself from teasing him. "Do you always use your badge to get dates?"

"Only with unusually obstinate women who have a tendency to end up at my crime scenes, then insist on helping me investigate."

I laughed. "Are you saying you run into those kinds of women regularly?"

He chuckled. "No, not until I came to Cumberpatch."

"It sounds to me as if the move has been good for you, then," I said.

The amber in his eyes darkened, and he brushed his fingertip along the back of my hand. "I'll admit it's been challenging, but most of it in a good way."

CHAPTER EIGHT

Logan's taller height made his legs longer, yet he slowed his pace, so our walk back to Mysterious Baubles wasn't rushed. It was almost as if he wasn't in a hurry for either of us to go back to work.

"I understand the festival this weekend is quite an event." Logan pushed back the edges of his jacket and tucked his hands in his pockets. "I take it you'll be attending."

"Yeah, my friends and I will be there, pirate costumes and all." I left out the part that we'd be searching for clues to Jake's murder, and probably have a ghost traipsing along with us.

Though I knew it was probably impossible, I hoped Martin's pranks would be minimal. The next time I saw the annoying spirit, I planned to utilize my clause for changing rules and tell him what he could and couldn't do in public when he was hanging out with my friends and me. Most of the emphasis would be on the couldn't list.

"A costume, huh." He grinned. "That does sound intriguing."

"Are you planning to attend the festivities as well?" I stopped next to him at the end of the sidewalk and waited for the pedestrian light to signal it was safe to cross the street.

He nodded. "I'll more than likely be there in an official capacity."

Now that our conversation had moved on to a safer topic, the tension I'd experienced earlier had faded. I'd even pushed aside my concerns about Martin making an unwanted appearance so we could continue his search for Pete. At least that's what I thought until a woman going in the opposite direction passed us on the sidewalk.

It wasn't the woman who caught my attention, but the large white bag she was carrying. More specifically, the bold letters for the "Cumberpatch Pirate Museum" printed on the plastic.

When I'd been composing a list of all the possible places to search for Pete's eye patch, I hadn't even considered checking out the museum. Excited by the possibility of resolving one of my mysteries, I decided not to put it off until later.

Once we'd crossed the street, we were on the same block as the shop, and not far from his truck. I placed my hand on his arm to stop him. "I hope you don't mind, but I remembered an errand I need to run before heading back to work."

"Sure, no problem." If Logan didn't believe me, he was keeping the opinion to himself. "I guess I'll see you this weekend."

It wasn't exactly a date, but knowing I'd see Logan again in a couple of days gave me something to look forward to and made my heart race.

After he turned and headed to his vehicle, I waited for him to pull into traffic before sending a text to Jade, letting her know what I planned to do. I'd barely received her enthusiastic response when I felt a chill along my arm, and Martin appeared beside me. He was wearing the same touristy outfit he'd had on the day before, but he'd replaced his laced sneakers with a pair of dark brown loafers.

"I believe the detective likes ye, Lass."

I pulled out my phone and held it to my ear so I could continue our conversation without attracting attention. "How did you…" I glanced past Martin, worried that Logan had returned. When I didn't see him or his vehicle anywhere, I knew there was only one way the ghost could have known we'd spent time together. "Please tell me you weren't spying on us."

Martin toed a crack in the sidewalk. "I might 'ave popped in fer a moment to see wha' ye were doin', but that was all."

"Uh-huh." I tamped down my irritation by reminding myself he'd been stuck in this world without anyone to talk to besides me for way too long. Since my destination was a couple of blocks away on the opposite side of the street, I headed for the nearest crosswalk.

"Do ye nah needs to return to work?" he asked.

"I have to go somewhere else first." I stopped again to wait for another light.

"Where be we off to, then?"

"I thought I'd stop by the pirate museum to see if they've gotten in any new displays recently." He seemed confused, so I added, "To see if they have any eye patches."

"That be a brilliant idea." He clasped his hands together, excitement flickering in his eyes.

By the time we reached the museum, I was getting tired of holding the phone to my head. "Before we go inside, I want you to promise me you will behave yourself. No touching *anything*, and especially no tricks." The objects inside the museum were priceless, and I didn't need him pulling things out of display cases like he did with his saber.

"I assure ye I shall be on me best behavior." He waved his hand toward the door waiting for me to enter. Once inside, he stopped to admire the life-sized portrait of himself hanging in the lobby.

"Quite a handsome chap, do ye not reckon?" Martin placed a hand on his hip and raised his head, mimicking the stance in the picture.

I clapped a hand over my mouth to stifle a giggle. As far as renderings went, it wasn't bad. Though the artist had failed to capture the devilish gleam in Martin's eyes.

I'd only taken a few steps when someone said my name. I turned toward the gift shop designed to look like the inside of a pirate ship. Ben Hoopler, one of Greg's employees, was standing behind the counter, his smile forming dimples on his rounded cheeks. An ample amount of hair product had been worked into his dark hair forming short spikes on the top of his head. Ben smoothed the front of his buttoned vest. "Are you here to take a tour? The next one doesn't start for another half hour."

"Actually, I was hoping to talk to Greg. Is he around?" I asked.

"Sure, he's in the back. Let me go get him for you." He walked around the counter and slipped underneath the velvety red rope strung between two posts blocking off the lobby from the main part of the building, and the large room housing all the museum artifacts.

It had been a few months since my last visit to the museum when I'd delivered brochures for the Founders Day festivities. At the time, my friends and I had assumed someone on the committee was responsible for Jessica's death. Greg Abernathy, the museum's owner, was on the list, and I'd used the opportunity to question him extensively. A conversation that left him slightly annoyed with me.

"Hey, Rylee." If Greg was still angry, it wasn't showing. His smile was friendly, and the tone of his voice sounded genuine. He waited for Ben to return to the gift shop, then urged me to follow him to the other side of the lobby. "What can I do for you?"

"I recently had a conversation with someone who knew quite a bit about our town's history. He mentioned that one of the members of Martin Cumberpatch's crew wore a jeweled eye patch."

Even though Martin had promised to behave himself, I wasn't going to let him out of my sight. After glancing around, I noticed that Martin had moved away from the entrance and was walking around the glass display cases, his arms behind his back.

Satisfied that he was keeping his word, I continued. "And since you're quite knowledgeable about all the pirates who sailed along our coast, I was wondering if you'd ever heard about it or happened to have it on display."

Greg scratched the top of his head. "Honestly, I've never come across any eye patches from that era or heard any stories about one containing jewels."

He might not be an expert, but Greg was knowledgeable when it came to our town's pirate lore. Even so, I'd done some of my own online research the night before. Unfortunately, the only information I could find mentioned Martin, his crew, and his ship the *Renegade's Revenge*.

There wasn't a single reference to Pete, and I was beginning to wonder if he'd really existed or if Martin had made up the story about his best mate as an elaborate joke to play on my friends and me.

I changed my mind after seeing the disappointed look on Martin's face seconds before he disappeared. I felt bad for the ghost and would have called him back to give him some reassuring words if I could have.

"How's Max doing?" Greg asked, interrupting my concerned thoughts. "I can't imagine having a murder occur near his boat would be good for business."

"You'd think that would be the case, but it's not. It seems quite a few of the tourists arriving early for the festival have a thing for dead bodies. His tours are fully booked for the next few days."

"Have you heard whether or not the police have any idea who did it yet?" he asked.

Greg dealt with a lot of people throughout the day, not all of them tourists. If I could keep him talking without annoying him, maybe I'd pick up another clue that might help my uncle. "Nothing yet, how about you?"

"I do know that Jake wasn't very well-liked. I imagine the police have a large number of suspects." He rubbed his chin. "I'll bet it gets even longer when they start investigating the people he hurt with some of his shady dealings."

"Really? What kind of shady dealings?" I'd have thought after hearing about all the things Jake did to hurt my uncle's business, I wouldn't be shocked, but I was.

Greg frowned. "The kind where he'd con someone into joining a business venture with him, then take their money."

I gasped. "That's terrible." It was a far better clue then the argument between Jake and Lucas. Curious to learn more, I leaned a little closer. "How did you hear about it?"

I was afraid I'd pushed too hard when Greg didn't answer right away. "When I first moved here, Jake approached me about becoming a silent partner for the museum, but I turned him down."

I got the impression there was more to the story. "Do you mind telling me why?"

Greg shook his head. "Not at all. When Jake told me about his proposal, I asked him if he could provide me with a list of references. He blew me off, telling me that his tour business was doing great, and that should be incentive enough to work with him."

"Is that when you told him no?" It's the response I would've given Jake if I'd been in the same situation.

"It was, but I still had a friend of mine who lives in Boston check out Jake and his company, anyway."

"And?"

"And nothing." Greg shrugged. "He couldn't find any information about Jake before he moved to Cumberpatch."

"That is kind of strange." Did that mean Jake had changed his name, or that he was using an alias? Surely Logan had done a more thorough background check on Jake. I wished I'd known the information before he'd taken me out for coffee. I would've tried to find out what he knew, and see if it made my uncle appear guiltier than he already did.

I remembered Shawna's comment about the spouse usually being the killer. Learning about Jake's unethical side made me suspicious of Arlene. How much did she know about her husband's other business dealings? Was it possible she found out something about his past, something she didn't want anyone else to know?

Or were Braden and Arlene also involved in the schemes Greg had mentioned? Was it possible that she had something going on with Braden, and the two of them decided they no longer needed Jake as a partner?

If that was the case, then Jake's murder had been the perfect opportunity to get him out of the picture. More importantly, had blaming Max been part of the plan, a way to get rid of the competition and mislead the police at the same time?

"Isn't it, though?" Greg said, then turned as the sound of muffled voices and footsteps signaled the end of the latest tour. "I'm afraid I need to go."

"No problem," I moved toward the door. "I appreciate you taking the time to answer my questions."

"My pleasure," he said, hurrying into the gift shop to help Ben.

Once outside, I headed back to the shop, wishing my trip to the museum had given me more than a lot of speculations and the beginnings of a headache.

CHAPTER NINE

With closing time a half-hour away and the last customer already gone, I told Jade she could leave early, and I'd finish restocking shelves. I pulled supplies out of a box I'd gotten from the storeroom and thought about the conversation I'd had with Greg. The more I pondered my current list of possible suspects, the more questions I had without answers.

Questions like how many people had Jake successfully swindled after he moved to Cumberpatch? Or, was it possible that someone from his past had tracked him down and had been pretending to be a tourist to finish him off? And why use my uncle's saber and leave the body near his boat? Why not take care of Jake on his own boat, or somewhere else altogether?

I was still going with the theory that whoever killed Jake had purposely wanted my uncle to be blamed for it. What continued to baffle me was who it could be and why. Max was well-liked by pretty much everyone, except for maybe Amanda. Their breakup had happened a long time ago. Would she really wait this long to exact some revenge? And, if so, what was her link to Jake?

I was hoping to share my thoughts with Shawna and

Jade when I met with them after work. I also wanted to catch them up on my unsuccessful search for Pete, and see if they had any helpful ideas.

Gathering information about Jake's case would be a lot easier if I could discuss it with Logan. He had the means to access that kind of information, but collaborating with me was definitely not on his agenda.

Since I wasn't in law enforcement and my amateur sleuthing skills came from reading fiction and watching television, finding answers was going to be difficult.

I'd even experienced a momentary lapse in good sense and considered having Grams and Mattie take Roy out for ice cream again to see if they could bribe him for any details about the case. The amount of trouble she'd cause if her efforts backfired and Logan found out my family and I were interfering in his case wasn't worth getting her involved.

Reviewing my never-ending list of questions was put on hold when I heard footsteps and the sound of my grandmother's voice. "Rylee, there's something I need to tell you."

"Sure, what is it?" I placed the two bottles of herbal remedies I was holding on the shelf in front of me.

"I want you to know it wasn't my fault, and I need you to promise me that you're not going to get upset when I tell you." Her pursed lips made the wrinkles around her eyes deepen.

Whatever it was had to be bad if she was making me promise not to get mad first. "What did you do?"

"Nothing." She glanced down and pretended to pick a piece of lint off her long, plaid skirt.

"Grams," I insisted.

She raised her head to hold my gaze again. "I'm sure you've already heard Josh is in town for the festival, and he's staying with Mattie."

I'd gotten the information from Max the day he'd stop by the shop, and I'd volunteered my help. I wasn't sure what Josh's visit had to do with what my grandmother wanted to tell me. "And." I wiggled my fingers, urging her to continue.

"You know I worry that you haven't been in a serious relationship since…"

"Yeah." Besides my aversion to discussing anything pertaining to the paranormal, the topic of my love life, or lack thereof, was something I avoided.

My family and friends had gotten good at not mentioning Hudson Bradley, my cheating jerk of an ex-boyfriend. The two years I'd wasted on a relationship I thought was going to last forever was not something I ever wanted to discuss again.

Luckily, he'd moved to Portland, sparing me constant reminders and keeping my father from searching for someone to put a hex on him. At the time my loving parent had made the offer, I didn't think it was possible. Now that I could see ghosts and knew Martin had been cursed, my views on the subject had changed considerably.

"Josh might have overheard part of Mattie and me talking about you finding a boyfriend."

I rubbed my forehead so hard I was sure it left a mark. Though I'd always suspected Grams discussed me with Mattie when I wasn't around, this was the first time she'd admitted it out loud. "Please tell me the two of you weren't discussing Logan."

"His name might have come up, but that's not the part Josh overheard," Grams said.

I narrowed my gaze even more. "What part did he hear, and why do I have a bad feeling I should be worried?"

"He thought we meant you needed a boyfriend and assumed we wanted him to ask you out." Grams talked as if she were competing in a rapid speech contest.

Too bad I was a good listener and hadn't missed a word she'd said. I groaned and clutched the edge of the shelf.

"We tried to talk him out of it, but you know how Josh gets."

I knew exactly what she meant. Josh was one of those guys that when he got an idea in his head, he wouldn't let go of it no matter how much someone tried to talk him out of it. And according to Mattie, his determination could get really annoying. Personally, I didn't know him that well. We'd had a handful of conversations over the years, and he'd always seemed harmless.

I remembered when Bryce formed the spoofers, and Josh wanted to become a member. He'd followed Bryce and his friends around for an entire summer vacation. Bryce told Jade it was the longest two weeks of his life, time he'd spent trying to avoid Josh, which was difficult because the guy kept showing up at their home.

With the festival still a few days off, the last thing I wanted was to have him shadowing me for the remainder of his visit. "Grams…" I didn't get a chance to tell her I was disowning her for life because the bell tinkled, and two middle-aged women walked into the shop.

"I'll take care of them." For an elderly woman, my grandmother could move fast.

I returned to stocking the shelves and tried to remember that what she did was because she cared. I probably would have forgiven her if Josh hadn't strolled into the shop a few minutes later. He was carrying a handful of flowers, a determined smile on his face.

If dumping out the remaining contents and covering my head with the box sitting near my feet would have kept him from noticing me, I would've done it.

"Rylee, I've missed you," he said, holding out a makeshift bouquet containing a couple of weeds, making me wonder which one of Mattie's neighbors he'd stolen the flowers from.

We weren't close friends, and I hadn't missed him in the slightest. "Hi, Josh," I muttered, refusing to take the flowers or reciprocate with a similar sentiment. I sidestepped his outstretched arms, barely escaping a hug. I thought about heading to the back of the store and putting the counter between us but was afraid he'd follow me, and then I'd be trapped.

"How have you been?" I wasn't interested but asked to be polite. Besides, I got plenty of updates from Mattie about her nephew's exploits.

"I've been doing great. I even got promoted to head cashier at the grocery store last week." He stuck out his chest as if finally getting a promotion after working at the same place for almost seven years was a great accomplishment.

"That's nice." I grabbed the box off the floor, then scooted around him and headed to the other end of the aisle to finish stocking shelves.

"You know what that means, right?" he asked.

"Nope." I didn't want to know, nor did I want to encourage him to continue the conversation. What I really wanted was for him to leave so I could go back to plotting the ways I was going to get even with my grandmother. Maybe even Mattie since she was guilty by association.

If I wasn't so fond of her cream cheese muffins, I'd be tempted to boycott buying anything from her shop for at least a week.

Surprisingly, when Martin appeared next to Josh, his arms crossed and scowling, I didn't jump. "If this bloke be botherin' ye, Lass, I would be happy to run 'im through fer ye." The glare Martin leveled at Josh made me think he was serious.

"What? No," I blurted, realizing my mistake too late.

Josh wrinkled his nose. "But I didn't ask you yet."

"Ask me what?"

"If you'd go with me to the Pirate Festival." He held the bouquet out again.

When Martin raised a brow, letting me know he was still willing to make good on his offer, I gave the meddling ghost my back. "Uh, gee Josh, I appreciate your thoughtfulness, but I'll be working all day." I'd be busy helping only if my uncle needed supplies, so it was partially the truth. I was also hoping to see Logan and didn't need Josh hanging around.

"That's okay." Josh smiled. "We can spend time together during your breaks."

CHAPTER TEN

When Shawna and Jade told me we were going to the corner grocery for snacks, they'd neglected to tell me they'd also planned to take me on a stakeout. One they didn't mention until we arrived in Arlene's neighborhood and had parked across the street from her house.

"Are there any more of those chocolates left that your mother sent from Las Vegas?" Jade turned in her seat and held out her hand expectantly.

"Sorry, we polished those off twenty minutes ago." It was a good thing my friends hadn't been around when I'd received the package; otherwise, the additional bag of colorful, delectable treasures I'd hidden in my desk would have disappeared along with the first one.

"I can't believe I let you guys talk me into this. Arlene already told Roy she thinks Max murdered her husband, and she's not exactly a fan of the rest of my family." I stared from my place in the backseat of Jade's car at the light filtering through the blind covering the front window of her home.

The house was a white two-story colonial with an attached two-car garage. There were four columns situated beneath an awning running along the front porch. The lawn was well-manicured, and flowerbeds lined the red brick walkway leading from the sidewalk to the first step.

Jade had parked across the street, but it didn't stop me from worrying that the police were going to show up any minute after receiving a report of suspicious characters lurking in the neighborhood.

"Don't you want to know if Braden and Arlene are involved?" Shawna shifted sideways to glance back at me. "We can't exactly follow them around during the day, not without making her suspicious."

My friend was the one who wanted to know if the two were having an affair. All I wanted to know was whether or not they were responsible for Jake's death, something I was certain I could find out during daylight hours.

"Yeah," I snorted. "I can see how three women sitting in a parked car in a quiet neighborhood late at night wouldn't seem unusual at all."

Shawna frowned, then grabbed a handful of chips out of the bag sitting between her and Jade. She stuffed them in her mouth, crunching them loudly as she turned to face forward again.

"Guys." Jade straightened in her seat, her voice rising with excitement. "It looks like this wasn't a waste of time after all."

I leaned forward to get a better look at the vehicle pulling into Arlene's driveway. As soon as the driver's door opened and the automatic light above the front door came on, the three of us gasped at the identity of the new arrival.

"Hey, isn't that…" Jade was the first to comment.

"Yep," I said.

"Well, I didn't see that coming." Shawna gripped the dashboard. "I guess Arlene likes younger guys."

"It appears so." I watched Arlene open the door with a huge smile, then pull Lucas into a tight hug. If they were in a close relationship, I'd have expected a full-blown kiss on the lips, not the chaste one she placed on his cheek.

As soon as Arlene moved out of the way, Lucas

hitched the backpack he was carrying over his shoulder and stepped inside. After glancing back and forth along the street as if checking to see if anyone was watching them, she trailed after him.

The second the door closed, I released the breath I was holding, glad Jade had parked next to some large trees and away from any street lamps.

"Do you think Lucas was really sick or that Arlene was the reason he missed two days of work?" Jade asked.

I wanted to believe Lucas had honestly been too sick to work, but it seemed too much of a coincidence to ignore. "Chloe did say she saw Lucas arguing with Jake a few days before we found him in the water."

"Do you think it's possible Jake found out what Lucas and Arlene were up to, and that's what the argument was about?" Jade asked.

"Maybe we should go ask him." Shawna reached for her door handle.

Jade grabbed the sleeve of Shawna's jacket before I could. "We can't just go knock on her door and start asking questions."

"Why not?" Shawna asked.

"Because we're not supposed to be here, remember." As soon as Shawna took her hand off the handle, Jade released her sleeve.

Relieved, I leaned back against the seat. "I'm with Jade. It's not like we can say, hey Arlene, we were in the neighborhood spying on you and had some questions. Do you mind if we come in?"

"Well, when you say it like that." Shawna harrumphed and crossed her arms. "Then what do you suggest we do to find out?"

"I believe I can help, Lass." Martin's bulky frame appeared next to me and filled up the remainder of the seat. His T-shirt was still the same, but he had on some khaki pants and an old pair of worn military-style boots.

"Not to ruin your fun, but do you suppose you could

start ringing a bell or something, instead of popping in and scaring the heck out of me?" I scooted closer to the door to keep from touching him. Spirits weren't known for being warm, and I was already chilled from sitting in the cold car. The nights were getting cooler, and to remain inconspicuous, Jade hadn't run the vehicle's heater.

Seemingly entertained by my request, he laughed. "I shall see wha' I can do."

"Martin's here." I told Jade and Shawna in answer to the inquisitive looks they were giving me. After what he'd done to Braden, I wasn't sure I wanted any more of his help and left out that part of our conversation.

"Inform yer friend that I 'ave confirmed that the Braden bloke ain't doin' it wit' the widow Arlene." It was too bad Shawna couldn't see Martin. She might have found the way he wiggled his bushy brows humorous.

"How do you know what Braden has been up to?" I asked.

"'cause I 'ave been followin' 'im."

It reminded me of how Jessica had followed an obnoxious tourist I'd met at the cemetery, who later turned out to be her killer. "Why would you do that?" I tried not to sound ungrateful or skeptical. Martin going places my friends and I couldn't was an asset, but I worried his propensity for causing trouble might make things worse.

"Since ye 'ave been workin' on yer end of our bargain, I felt it only fair that I do the same," Martin said.

After everything I'd learned in history class, having honor was not something I associated with pirates, yet every now and then, Martin demonstrated that he had some.

"What did he say?" Shawna asked.

"He said Braden and Arlene aren't together." Which we'd just discovered. "He also said he's been following Braden."

"Oooh, that could be helpful. Maybe we should have

him follow Lucas as well." Shawna smiled and continued to look at the empty space where Martin was sitting.

"That might not be a bad idea." Jade gave Shawna a supportive nod. "But first, we need to know if he found out anything interesting about Braden, something that might help Max."

I glanced at Martin, waiting for him to answer.

"Thar was somethin', but I dunno if 'twould be helpful," Martin said.

"Really, what?" At this point, I'd take even the smallest clue.

Martin tugged at the hairs on his chin. "He was speakin' into a phone thin' like yers 'n sounded mighty angry at whoever he was talkin' to."

"Did Braden mention a name?"

He shook his head. "Nah that I recall?"

A name would have made things easier, but I wasn't ready to give up. "Could you tell what they were arguing about?" I asked.

"Braden told the person he was speakin' wit' they needed to keep their part of the deal, or they was goin' to be sorry."

I repeated what Martin said to Jade and Shawna.

"It's not much to go on," Jade said.

"Yeah, and it could have been anyone on the other end of the line. Even someone Braden does business with." Shawna scrunched up her empty chip bag and tossed it on the floor. "I'll clean it up later, I promise," she said before Jade reprimanded her for messing up her car.

"So much for a new lead." Silence followed my comment and I stared out the window contemplating other possibilities.

"Did you see that?" Jade pointed at Arlene's house. The lights on the lower level went dark, replaced by new ones on the upper-level a short time later. "I guess Lucas must be spending the night."

"Do you think we should have Martin…" Jade and I

cut off Shawna's suggestion with an emphatic no at the same time.

I wanted to know if Arlene and Lucas were involved in Jake's murder even more than my friends did, but I respected privacy, whether it was mine or someone else's. "I think we should call it a night and regroup tomorrow."

Jade started the engine. "I'm in total agreement with that plan."

CHAPTER ELEVEN

After my first, and hopefully last late-night stakeout, I'd gotten a few hours of sleep before getting up early for work. I'd also made it through a busy morning at the shop without any unusual incidences or new relationship-related revelations from my grandmother.

Shortly after our arrival, Barley had magically ended up in his pirate costume again. For some reason, he didn't seem to mind and was enjoying the extra attention he received from all our customers.

I remembered Max telling me he'd purchased Martin's saber from the Booty Bizarre. There was a chance Hildie Simpkins, the owner, also had Pete's eye patch or knew where I might be able to find it. Since Shawna was working and I needed Jade to cover for me, I'd convinced Martin to go with me and help identify the patch.

I stood on the sidewalk staring through the shop's storefront window with my cell pressed to my ear. I wasn't much of a shopper and the last time I'd visited the place I'd been searching for an unusual birthday gift for my mother. The inside was filled with old treasures and hadn't changed much.

I watched Martin, trying to decipher what he was

thinking. His expression was a combination of trepidation and anxiousness. He'd been trapped with his saber for a long time, and I had no idea how much of it had been spent locked away inside Hildie's store. So far, our search had been disappointing, and if roles were reversed, I'd probably be nervous about entering the store too.

I didn't want to be responsible for causing him any additional trauma. "I'll understand if you don't want to go inside."

"I appreciate yer concern, Lass, but I shall be fine. I wishes to do whatever be necessary to find me best mate." His forced smile didn't reach his concerned gaze. "'n I promise to behave meself."

I had to give him credit for being a lot braver than I would've been. "Okay, then." I reached for the door handle, slipping my phone into my pocket as I walked inside.

Shortly after a bell similar to the one in my family's shop announced my arrival, I scanned the cluttered room and spotted Hildie peeking her head out from behind a tall cabinet.

She was in her mid-forties and had short brown hair layered to accent her heart-shaped face. Her smile made her rounded cheeks seem more prominent. She'd inherited the store when her grandfather passed away a few years ago, and as far as I knew, her business was doing well.

"Hey, Rylee, I'll be right with you."

I returned her smile, then waited for her to place a figurine on a glass shelf filled with all kinds of antiques. After securing the latch on the door, she made her way around a Victorian-style chair and a table covered with three different types of china. "What can I do for you?"

"I'm looking for something for my uncle." Since Max had purchased Martin's saber from her store and was always looking for other pirate-related items, it was a believable fib. On the walk over here, I'd thought about telling her the gift was for my father, but everything he collected revolved around the paranormal, a fact that was well-known amongst the people in town who knew him.

"Did you have something specific in mind?" She waved her hand through the air. "I have quite a selection, and I'm sure we'll be able to find him the perfect gift."

"I do." I reached into my purse and pulled out a folded piece of paper. I wasn't much of an artist, but I'd done a basic sketch of Pete's eye patch based on Martin's description to show her. "Do you have any eye patches that look like this?"

Hildie took the drawing and examined it closely. I could tell by the way she was scrutinizing the picture that she was struggling with my rendering.

"Why don't I show you what I have?" She handed it back, opting for being polite rather than providing a critique.

"That would be great." I tried not to let my excitement seep into my voice.

Hildie was a shrewd salesperson and paid close attention to people's reactions while they were shopping. Most of the items in the store didn't have price tags attached to them. I wasn't made of money, and if she gleaned how badly I wanted this particular eye patch, she might be inclined to raise the price.

If she did have the patch I needed, there was a slim chance no purchasing would be required. I was a novice when it came to understanding the extent of my ghost seeking abilities and wasn't sure how everything worked. I hoped that once I found the patch, all I had to do was touch it like I had Martin's saber, and Pete's spirit would be freed.

Martin had been listening to my conversation with Hildie and seemed more anxious than I was. He'd stopped perusing the selection of weapons in a glass case near the front of the store, and followed us.

"I heard about what happened to Jake." Hildie paused to glance at me over her shoulder. "There are even rumors going around that Max is responsible." She winced at my intimidating glare. "Not that I believe them."

I bit back the words "yeah right" and continued to follow her. She walked around several more chairs, then stopped in front of a display case on the opposite side of the room. Several shelves filled with books, their spines old and worn, lined the wall behind the display. A handful of books pertained to the supernatural, their titles referencing magic. A few others were thick and looked as if they contained the complete history for Cumberpatch Cove and the surrounding area.

"Any idea what the police plan to do with the saber once they arrest the killer?" Hildie asked.

"I have no idea." Up until now, I hadn't given any thought to whether or not the police returned belongings, especially those used in a murder, once they sent the criminals to jail. I did find it strange that she seemed more concerned about what happened to the blade than finding out who actually committed the murder.

Now that there was a considerable amount of notoriety attached to the saber, its worth might have increased substantially. Maybe Hildie was thinking about buying it back from Max so she could resell it to a collector willing to pay a lot more money for it. He was already convinced the saber belonged to Martin, which it did. Murder weapon or not, I didn't think he'd be willing to sell it at any price.

"Well, anyway, here's what I have." She pointed at the wooden shelf beneath the glass counter.

It was hard not to miss the blade that looked almost identical to Martin's laying on a bed of velvety blue material next to the patches. I leaned closer to get a better look. "That looks just like the saber Max bought."

"It's a replica. My cousin, who lives in Portland, makes them for me. You'd be surprised how many of them I sell during the festival, and for a decent profit," she said with smug satisfaction.

Actually, I wasn't surprised at all. Pirate paraphernalia

was popular this time of year. It was the reason I made sure my family's shop was well-stocked.

Martin pressed his nose close to the glass. "She be tellin' the truth. 'Tis a fake 'n a fairly decent one at that." He straightened to grin at me. "Mine has me mark etched on the blade below the hilt."

"Were you interested in buying one for yourself?" Hildie asked.

"No, it's the patches I came for." I shifted my attention back to the other side of the case. It was easy to see by their worn leather edges that they were old and had been used frequently. One of them was in such bad shape I was afraid it would unravel at the seams the next time it was handled. "I don't see any with a jewel worked into the leather."

"Oh, is that what that dark spot was supposed to be?" Hildie asked, then clasped her hand over her mouth, realizing what she'd said out loud.

I knew I lacked artistic skills and wasn't insulted by her honesty. "It's okay." I gave her arm a gentle pat and laughed. "My stick people drawings aren't much better either."

She tapped the glass with her fingernail. "I don't recall ever having any patches with jewels sewn into the leather before, but that doesn't mean my grandfather didn't sell one."

With all the tourists that visited Cumberpatch, Pete's eye patch could be anywhere. For all I knew, a collector from another state could have purchased it. "I don't suppose he kept records of all his sales, did he?"

"I'm afraid not, but I could give you the name of a collector I know in Bangor who might have seen one and be able to help you. That is unless you think Max would be interested in one of these." She gave me an eager smile, no doubt hoping she'd still make a sale.

"The collector's information would be great, thank you."

Though disappointment flickered in her gaze, she kept her tone pleasant. "I'll be right back, the information is in my office." She turned and headed toward the back of the shop.

Martin's shoulders slumped even more than they did during our visit with Greg. It was upsetting to see him so disheartened. I was disappointed and wished I could give him a hug.

It didn't take long for Hildie to return and hand me one of her business cards. "The number is on the back."

"Thanks, I appreciate it."

"Sure," she said, curtly dismissing me to hurry across the room and assist a new customer.

I tucked the card in my pocket and headed for the door. I was relieved Martin had decided to follow me instead of doing one of his disappearing acts. Once we were outside, I pulled out my cell so I could talk to him.

"I'm not giving up yet. There has to be another way to find Pete." Of course, I had no idea what that other way might be, but I was determined to figure it out.

Martin widened his eyes and stopped dragging his feet. "Do ye really reckon so?"

"I do." I headed back toward my family's shop, contemplating what to do next. Other than doing a worldwide Internet search, I'd exhausted all the ideas for any local exploration that I could come up with. It looked like I was going to have to ask the spoofers for help, after all.

CHAPTER TWELVE

The sun was setting by the time I closed the shop, and Shawna, Grams, and I had piled into Jade's car for our latest excursion. Now that my grandmother knew about the quest to help Martin, preventing her from helping us was moot. She'd insisted that her yet to be proven psychic abilities might come in handy with finding Pete.

One of my parents' stipulations, when they'd left me in charge of the shop, was to make sure Grams didn't get into any trouble. If she was hanging out with my friends and me, I wouldn't need to worry about her doing any sleuthing on her own. She'd already informed me that she and Mattie had taken Roy a basket of muffins, trying to gain information about his and Logan's investigation.

Roy and Grams had been friends for years, though I sometimes suspected Roy would like it to be more. The sheriff was intelligent and probably knew what the two women were doing. It would explain why they didn't have much luck finding out anything new about the investigation.

I couldn't shake the feeling that whoever used the saber to kill Jake either had a grudge against my uncle or wanted him to take the blame. Since the display case where he'd kept the weapon had been locked when my friends and I found the body, was it possible the culprit also knew Martin's blade showed up in odd places on the *Buccaneer's Delight*?

I could only deal with one problem at a time and needed to focus my energies on helping Martin. Thinking about the pirate reminded me that I hadn't seen him all day. Even though I'd promised him I'd keep helping, I wondered if he was off sulking because of yesterday's disheartening visit to the Booty Bizarre. Or maybe he'd found someone else to follow like he had Braden. After everything my friends and I had discussed with him during our stakeout, Lucas and Arlene would be my obvious choices.

Finding answers to my questions would have to wait because we'd arrived at Bryce's place. He had been more than a little excited when I'd called and asked for his help. We'd barely made it out of the car when he rushed out onto the front porch with Nate and Myra following close behind him.

"Hey, guys. I'm glad you could make it. Come on inside." With a huge grin and a wave of his hand, Bryce ushered us toward the door.

When Nate took Shawna's hand after holding the door open for her, Bryce frowned. He noticed me watching, then quickly masked his expression, further confirming mine and Jade's suspicions that he had an unrequited thing for Shawna, one he had yet to act upon.

I hadn't been to Bryce's home for a long time. Normally, when I ran into him, it was during one of his visits to Jade and Shawna's place. He lived in a one-story ranch style house painted a spruce green with off-white shutters and trim around all the windows. The interior walls were all a light tan with basic furniture situated on a dark carpet in the living room.

Bryce spent most of his time reading books or in front of a computer. Even so, he had decent housekeeping skills and kept his place tidy.

"Our clubhouse, I mean headquarters, is this way." Bryce made it sound as if he was leading us to a secret facility and not the closed door on the other side of his kitchen.

If he was trying to create a spooky atmosphere, he'd done a great job. The lighting above the staircase leading into his basement was dim. Bryce, Myra, and Nate didn't hesitate to descend into darkness. Grams and Jade were the next to follow, but Shawna stopped in the entryway, refusing to go any farther. "Rylee, since this was your idea, I think you should go first," she said.

I pinned her with a disbelieving glare. I couldn't believe she didn't have a problem traipsing through a scary cemetery at night, yet she froze when it came to basements. "We'll go together." Without giving her a choice, I slipped my arm through hers and tugged her onto the first step.

With each creak of the wooden stairs, my grip on the handrail tightened, and the urge to leave heightened. It was a good thing I had sleeves and Shawna kept her nails short; otherwise, the skin on my arm would be covered with numerous indentations.

"If we get down there and Bryce has anything closely resembling a dead body, I'm out of here," Shawna muttered when we'd reach the halfway point.

"Trust me, I'll be right behind you." My nervous laugh might have sounded like I was kidding, but I was serious.

I was glad when we reached the bottom step and didn't find anything remotely resembling a corpse. Other than a washer and dryer sitting off to the side in a corner, the room resembled a modified office and mini living room. There was even a sofa large enough to fit three people and a couple of matching chairs. In the middle of one wall was an old laminated desk, the cushions on the chair sitting next to it were worn and faded. His computer system, on the other hand, appeared to be a state-of-the-art model.

My jacket helped with the basement's cooler temperature, but it didn't keep me from shivering when a wave of cold air preceded Martin's arrival. Already dealing with a high anxiety level, I jumped and squeaked when he touched my arm and said my name.

Shawna giggled, and Nate joined her. "Rylee, you look like you've seen a ghost."

Martin chuckled. "Yer friend's sense of humor be quite amusin'."

I should have known it would only be a matter of time before one of my friends thought it would be fun to use that particular comment. Even so, I scowled at Shawna. "Yeah, she's hilarious."

"I take it, Martin's here." Jade made herself comfortable in one of the chairs.

"Yeah," I glanced at the expectant faces around the room. Everyone except Myra, who'd crossed her arms and pressed her lips together tightly, seemed happy to hear the news.

Bryce clapped his hands together, his eyes widening with excitement. "Great, then let's get started."

By the way he was acting, I'd bet anything the spoofers rarely got asked to find cursed spirits or any other paranormal requests for that matter. They were the only non-magical option I had left to help Martin and return to my ghost-free existence, so I wasn't about to complain.

"He be quite the boisterous chap, be he nah?" Judging by Martin's wrinkled nose, I didn't think his comment was a compliment. "Are ye sure we can trust them?" His skeptical gaze hopped from Bryce to Myra.

Martin didn't include Nate in his perusal, so I assumed he'd already met with approval during our lunch at Ye Olde Angler. "Bryce, yes," I whispered. "The other one…" I shrugged.

I understood why he might be suspicious of Myra. She'd been clear how unimpressed she was with my friends and me, and had been glaring, mostly at me, as if we were unwelcome invaders since we'd arrived.

Myra's eyes narrowed even more. Either she had enhanced hearing, which I doubted, or she figured out I'd been talking about her.

Bryce walked over to the shelves lined with all kinds of books referencing paranormal topics ranging from how to summon a demon to a guide on how to use magical stones. He ran his fingertip across several titles, then pulled out one with a worn black leather binding and red lettering along its spine.

After carefully setting it on his desk as if it was his most prized possession, he hummed as he gently leafed through the pages. Once he found what he was looking for, he stepped aside so I could see the page he'd selected. "Ask Martin if this is Pete's eye patch." He pointed at a black and white image at the top of the page.

Martin was standing right next to me, so instead of repeating Bryce's request, I gave him an inquiring glance.

"Aye, that be the very one." His enthusiastic reply surpassed Bryce's earlier display and made me wince.

"He said that's it." I was relieved we were making progress, but realized I'd forgotten to ask Bryce earlier if Nate had mentioned the witch-related problem associated with finding the eye patch. It wouldn't be right not to let him know that helping me could have magical ramifications.

I leaned closer to the desk so I could get a better look at the text below the picture. "Does it say anything about the curse?" There was a chance Bryce had already read the book and might know the answer.

"Curse?" Myra hopped off the stool where she'd been sitting with her arms crossed, seemingly uninterested in our conversation up until now. "Nobody said anything about a curse."

"Rylee's been doing okay since she touched Martin's saber, so we believe it's more about breaking a spell, then actually getting cursed." Jade kept her voice calm as she placed a warning hand on Shawna's arm to keep her seated on the sofa, and prevent her from getting into an argument with Myra.

My friends were great at showing their support, but I could always count on Jade more than Shawna to use diplomacy and a level head when dealing with tension-filled situations.

"Oh, yeah, how's that?" Myra asked.

At the moment, I was more worried about the wary look Martin was giving her and what he might decide to do about. While keeping an eye on him, I quickly explained everything that had happened after touching his saber, including my visit to the Booty Bazaar and the pirate museum.

"It sounds like Jade's assessment of the situation might be correct. If Rylee is the only one who will be touching the eye patch, and has the ability to break the curse, then I don't think the rest of us have anything to be concerned about." Nate settled farther into the cushions and draped his arm across the back of the sofa behind Shawna.

I gave everyone a hopeful glance. "Does that mean you're all willing to help us find Pete?"

"I am," Nate said.

"Me too." Bryce joined Nate in staring at Myra.

Unable to withstand the pressure any longer, Myra huffed, "Fine, I'm in, but I think Rylee should talk to Joyce and Edith first. If there's magic involved, then they might know someone in the local coven who can help."

I'd always wondered if there were witches living in Cumberpatch, and if they'd formed a local coven. My curiosity spiked even more after meeting Martin. I'd even considered whether or not the witch who'd cursed him had descendants that might still be around. Did witches hold grudges? And, if they did, was it passed on from one generation to the next?

"Do ye reckon askin' witches fer help be a good idea?" A hint of fear laced Martin's voice, his ghostly skin paled, and he shuddered.

My experiences with the paranormal to date hadn't exactly been pleasant, and I'd be nervous too if I'd suffered through a curse. Finding Pete was only one of the many questions I had for Joyce and Edith, and procrastinating wasn't going to get me any answers.

"Myra's right." Though I hated to admit it. "I'll stop by the Classic Broom tomorrow."

CHAPTER THIRTEEN

I balanced the box containing face painting kits and small net style bags of chocolates shaped like coins and sealed with gold foil on my hip, then closed the hood on the trunk of my car. As much as I wanted to help Martin find Pete, I still needed to follow up on what Jade, Shawna, and I had discovered about Arlene and Lucas during our stakeout.

I didn't have any real proof that Lucas and Arlene had conspired to get rid of Jake because he learned about their affair. Heck, other than witnessing their hug and the friendly kiss Arlene had given Lucas on her front porch, I had no proof there was even anything going on between them.

I did, however, think having a conversation with Lucas about his argument with Jake deserved some follow-up, and Max calling me first thing in the morning asking me to bring him more supplies gave me a great opportunity.

Not only was business picking up because of the upcoming festival, but people were booking tours just for the chance to get a glimpse of where Jake was murdered. Max was a great storyteller, and I wouldn't be surprised if he was spinning an embellished tale at the beginning of every tour.

Of course, my side trip to see my uncle also gave me a justifiable reason to put off my visit with Joyce and Edith until later in the day.

When I reached the shop, Max was standing inside near the doorway chatting with Chloe. Instead of interrupting their conversation, I lifted the box and tipped my head toward the boat to let him know I was going to put the supplies away first. After getting a wave from Chloe and an acknowledging nod from my uncle, I hurried to finish my task.

The boat had been empty when I'd arrived, and I knew it wouldn't be long before the rest of Max's crew showed up to prep for the next tour. I had just finished stocking the depleted storeroom shelves when the room echoed with the sound of overhead footsteps.

Grabbing my empty box, I headed back to the deck. I was glad to see Lucas coming down the narrow staircase at the same time I started up them. It saved me the trouble of tracking him down to ask my questions.

"Hey, Rylee." He glanced at the box and smiled. "Oh good, you brought us more supplies." He shifted the sword tucked into the dark red sash tied around his waist as he turned and went back up the stairs, so I could finish my trek to the deck.

Several strands of blond hair had escaped from the leather tie at his nape, and he nervously tucked them behind his ear. "Thanks for covering for me while I was out. Chloe said you did a great job." He held his fist to his mouth to stifle a cough. The lingering signs of a recent cold proved he hadn't faked being sick.

He seemed fine and probably wasn't contagious anymore, but I kept a few feet between us anyway. "Not a problem. I was just glad my uniform still fit."

He smiled and eased toward the staircase, a sure sign he wanted to leave without being rude. "I understand you guys have been busy," I blurted out the first thing I could think of to make him stay. "Do you think it's because of the murder?"

"Yeah, maybe." His frown deepened.

"I heard the police talked to everyone who was here that day." My window for questioning him was rapidly getting smaller, so I risked being pushy. "Did they ask you about the argument you had with Jake? How about your relationship with Arlene?" When Lucas's eyes widened with shock and his body tensed, I regretted not being more subtle.

"How did you…" he stammered. "Yes, they did, but it's not what you think."

"It's not?" If I hadn't been holding the box, I would have crossed my arms to appear more intimidating. Turns out, it wasn't necessary.

"I do tarot readings in my spare time." Lucas nervously glanced toward the empty ramp leading to the dock before continuing. "Jake doesn't, I mean didn't believe in the paranormal and got upset when he found out I was doing readings for Arlene. That's what the argument was about, I swear. You can even ask Arlene if you don't believe me. I was at her house the other night."

"So you and Arlene aren't…"

Lucas wrinkled his nose. "Heck no. She's way too old for me."

"Rylee, are you still up here?" I heard heavy footsteps before Max appeared at the top of the ramp.

Lucas's face flushed, and he lowered his voice. "You're not going to tell him, are you? I really like working here and can't afford to lose this job."

I wasn't sure if he was referring to his side business or his association with Arlene. Since Grams also did tarot readings, I was leaning toward the latter. "I'm sure he's not going to care." I reassured him with a grin. "But if it makes you feel any better, he won't hear it from me."

"Thanks, I really appreciate it," Lucas said, then headed for the stairs.

As soon as he disappeared, I walked over and gave Max a hug. "Your shelves are full, but I can bring more supplies if you think you'll need them."

"I'll keep an eye on them and let you know."

"Do you mind if I ask you a personal question?" I asked when he stepped aside so I could leave.

"Not at all."

"I know you had problems with Jake trying to steal your customers, but did you know about his other shady business dealings?"

Max scratched his jaw. "If you're talking about his attempts to get people to partner with him, then yes, I knew. He approached me when he first moved to town, but I refused. It's probably why he put so much effort into being a pain in my backside."

"Did you also know he approached Greg Abernathy?"

"I hadn't heard, but I'm not surprised." He narrowed his gaze. "What's with all the interest in Jake?"

"Um…" I bit my lip.

He placed his hands on his hips. "You're not going around asking people questions because the police think I might be involved, are you?"

Unlike me, who'd panicked when Logan told me he thought I had something to do with Jessica's death, Max didn't seem upset to know he was considered a suspect.

"Rylee, does Grams know what you're doing?" he asked.

When it came to my family, one answer always led to more questions, so remaining silent was always best. At least I thought it did until he groaned. "Of course, she does." He pinched the bridge of his nose. "Please tell me she hasn't made another one of her predictions."

"Well, no, but…" I backed closer to the ramp.

"No buts about it," he said. "Getting involved is dangerous. The killer could be anyone, and I think you two should let Roy handle it."

His lecture was cut short by the sound of voices coming from the walkway below. With any luck, they were passengers for the next tour and would keep him busy.

"I'll make sure to let Grams know what you said." After flashing him a triumphant smile, I waved goodbye and made my escape down the ramp.

CHAPTER FOURTEEN

I arrived at the Classic Broom early, hoping to visit with Edith and Joyce before they got busy with customers. While I paused outside to mentally review the list of questions I planned to ask them, my gaze was drawn to the store's front door. The name of the shop, along with a witch flying on a broom beneath it, were intricately carved into the dark wood.

The place didn't seem as ominous as it had the last time I was here, but I was still reluctant to go inside. Maybe it was the store itself that made me wary. Or maybe the source of my tension stemmed from having to speak with Edith and Joyce. It was uncanny how the sisters knew things. Things that went beyond being exceptionally perceptive.

"Ye nah be goin' in thar, are ye?" Martin had joined me on the sidewalk, his somber mood getting worse the longer he examined the door.

"You're a ghost." I shot him a disapproving glance. "What do you have to be afraid of?" I was the mere human who lacked any useful magical abilities, not that I'd want any powers if someone offered them to me.

"Witches cast spells 'n curses. They can nah be

trusted." He crossed his arms. "Wha' if the women ye be meetin' 'ave the power to send me to the otherworld afore we find Pete?"

The Haverston sisters might offer psychic predictions, but I was pretty sure making unusual potions and candies was the extent of their abilities. They hadn't been able to do anything for Jessica when she was haunting me, so I didn't think they had the power to ship Martin off to another realm either.

"First off, I don't know for sure that Edith and Joyce are actually witches." I raised my hand when he opened his mouth to argue. "And if they are, I don't think they have those kinds of powers." Jessica had shown the same trepidation, had refused to go inside, the one and only time I'd sought their help. "Look, I'm not thrilled about going inside either, but this is our last option if we want to find Pete." I raised a challenging brow and reached for the door handle. "I'll understand if you want to cower out here on the sidewalk."

"I shall 'ave ye know I 'ave ne'er cowered in me life, 'n I do nah plan to start now," Martin ranted as he followed me inside.

"Okay." I closed the door behind us, ignoring the loud thud it made.

Martin stopped fuming long enough to glance around the shop, then glare at me. "Ye tricky wench, ye provoked me on purpose."

I grinned at how easily I'd coerced him. "Hey, no one said you had to come inside. You can leave whenever you want, but I'd like it if you stay. Edith and Joyce might have questions that only you can answer."

Other than a shelf now filled with what looked like voodoo dolls, the place hadn't changed a bit. The overhead lights were dimmed, creating a spooky ambiance.

Now that Martin was inside and could see for himself that there wasn't an unsuspecting witch ready to cast a spell on him, he seemed to be a little braver. He walked over to the nearest display case and perused the unusual items inside. "Did ye know they 'ave love potions in here?" He pointed at the wide assortment of colored bottles filled with liquid.

They also had wart removal and candy for broken hearts, if I remembered correctly. I was getting good at reading his facial expressions and recognized the desire to cause havoc immediately. "Don't even think about it."

"But Lass, would ye nah like to 'ave a wee bit of fun wit' that Lavender wench?"

"Maybe some other time." It was difficult to keep my interest masked. The thought of treating Lavender to some of Martin's mischief was tempting, but the fun would be short-lived. Messing with the woman gained the same results as provoking a rattlesnake, not something I recommended. Not when I was still waiting to see what kind of backlash I'd be dealing with from Trudy's witchy proclamation.

"Rylee, it's so good to see you." Edith emerged from a doorway on the left, then swept across the room. Her long black skirt billowed as she walked, and the absence of footsteps or even a creak on the hardwood floor was unnerving. She glanced around the room, her crystal blue eyes narrowing on the spot where Martin was standing. "And who were you talking to?"

Martin froze but didn't disappear like I'd expected. "I…"

"I'd like to know as well." Joyce swept into the room, her smile welcoming, her unusual entrance no less concerning. Other than the blood-red shawl draped over her shoulders, her dark outfit was similar to Edith's. Her eyes were the same sparkling shade of blue as her sisters, but her dark brown waist-length hair was a contrast to Edith's long blonde strands. "I'm assuming from the chill in the air that you were accompanied by a spiritual visitor."

"Jessica's not back, is she?" Edith asked. "Was there a problem with her staying in the afterlife?"

The possibility of spirits returning from their ghostly realm was disconcerting. I knew Grams was convinced that my great-great uncle Howard made random visits in the form of small animals whenever one of us needed help, but I'd never truly believed her predictions. "No, not that I know of. My visitor is a lot older and somewhat famous." The last part of my statement brought a wide grin to Martin's face.

"Really? That sounds interesting." Joyce rubbed her hands together.

"Yes, it does." Edith shared a knowing look with her sister, then returned her attention to me.

"Who is it?" they said in unison.

"Believe it or not, it's Martin Cumberpatch."

Joyce gasped. Edith muttered, oh my, then asked, "Are you sure?"

I bobbed my head. "I'm sure all right." I didn't take her disbelief personally. I'd had a hard time believing it was him myself when we'd first met.

"Well, then." Joyce's shock transformed into intrigue. "You need to tell us how this transpired and don't leave out any details."

I was getting tired of repeating the story and spent the next five minutes telling the sisters everything they wanted to know. I started with the way I'd been zapped by Martin's saber and how he'd appeared on Max's boat. Martin interrupted me a couple of times, insisting I provide additional details about his prankster exploits with the water cannons, which of course, I didn't think were necessary.

When I told Joyce and Edith what he'd said about his curse, he leaned against the counter listening intently, so I assumed I'd relayed the information correctly. I'd also expected a surprised reaction from the sisters; instead, I got a tsk from Joyce and a headshake from Edith.

"Through the years, there's been a lot of speculations made about how Martin disappeared, but nothing anyone in the magical community could prove," Edith said. "The local coven forbid anyone from talking about it."

"I don't understand. Why wouldn't they want anyone to know what really happened to Martin?" I asked.

"Those kinds of rumors are bad for business," Joyce said. "Tourists love the paranormal, but they aren't going to buy from someone who can cast a wicked spell on them."

That explained why nothing appeared in the town's history books. I thought of Shawna and her quest to turn an old boyfriend into a frog. Of course, that was when we were teenagers, but I had a feeling my friend wouldn't pass on the temptation if she learned it was available, and she'd had her heartbroken again.

"I know you were hoping the magic you acquired from the spirit seeker was temporary, but from what you've told us, it appears to be permanent," Joyce said.

"And since you were able to break Martin's curse, it must have given you additional spirit related powers." Edith shared an envious glance with her sister.

Having them confirm what I'd already concluded didn't make accepting my unwanted ability any easier. Hearing I'd received extra powers was even more troubling, but what worried me the most was not knowing what else might pop up in the future.

"There is an upside," Edith said when I frowned.

I knew the sisters thought my ability to see ghosts was a special gift, but being spirit free was the only positive thing that came to mind. "And what would that be?" I didn't want to be rude and forced the sarcasm from my voice.

The way she rolled her eyes reminded me of the silent scoldings I received from Grams whenever I struggled with figuring out the obvious. "You only have to deal with one spirit at a time."

"Edith's right." Joyce patted her sister's shoulder. "Could you imagine what it would be like if you had a cemetery full of ghosts following you around?"

Just thinking about the awful possibility had my stomach knotting. "Well, when you put it like that..."

"It is curious, though, that Martin continues to haunt you. I would have thought he'd move on once the curse was broken." Edith's contemplative gaze drifted in Martin's direction.

"I was wondering the same thing myself." Joyce crossed her arms and joined her sister in staring at the space where Martin was standing.

Martin's yellow T-shirt started to glow as he pushed away from the counter. "Did I nah warn ye they would try to send me on me way?"

"Martin, no one is sending you..." He vanished before I got a chance to finish.

"Is everything all right?" Joyce asked.

"No," I groaned. "Martin was afraid you were going to cast him into the afterlife, so he left."

"Oh, dear." Edith clasped a hand over her mouth.

"I'm afraid that's not how it works, not if he has unfinished business," Joyce said.

"Exactly," Edith agreed. "Did he happen to mention why he refuses to leave?"

"He told me his best friend, Pete, was also cursed."

"I see. Well, that does present a bit of a problem," Joyce said.

"Indeed." Edith bobbed her head in agreement.

"That's why I'm, I mean we were here. I've looked for Pete's eye patch everywhere in town I could think of and haven't been able to find it." I nervously shifted my weight from one foot to the other. I'd reached the point where I feared using mystical powers, something I had limited knowledge about, was the only way we'd be able to find Pete.

Unlike my father, who could write a book about the paranormal, I was out of my realm and didn't know if it was considered polite to ask the Haverston sisters if they were witches, let alone if they possessed any powers. "I was hoping you'd be able to help us."

"I assume the eye patch was Pete's personal item?" Joyce asked.

"Yeah." I glanced at some of the nearby display cases, then as a hopeful afterthought, I asked, "You don't happen to have any do you?"

"No, I'm afraid not, but that doesn't mean we can't find it another way." Joyce clasped the ends of her shawl as she stepped around the counter near their cash register and came back with a cell phone. "From what I understand, dealing with binding magic is tricky."

"I agree, it can be difficult and requires someone with a lot of experience. Since it also revolves around the dead, we might need a necromancer," Edith said, then hovered next to Joyce as she scrolled her finger along the screen of her phone.

You didn't grow up with my father without having heard the term mentioned once or twice. It was believing someone who could raise spirits from their resting place existed, and actually lived in Cumberpatch, that I was having a hard time accepting.

When Joyce stopped scrolling, Edith grinned and said, "Excellent choice."

"I thought so." Joyce tapped whatever number they'd agreed upon and placed her phone next to her ear.

"Good morning, Deeann." Joyce smiled and nodded. "Everything is fine." She listened for a few more seconds. "Do you remember Jonathan Spencer's daughter Rylee?" Another pause. "Yes, she requires our help." She paced in front of some nearby shelves, adjusting items as she told Deeann about Martin.

I wasn't happy that another person now knew I could see ghosts. At least Joyce kept her explanation to the specifics of what we needed to help Martin, not sharing how I'd gotten my powers or my previous experience with Jessica.

My scowl hadn't gone unnoticed by Edith. "Don't worry." She gave my arm a gentle squeeze. "Deeann will be discreet."

"I'll ask," Joyce stopped and turned in my direction. "Did Martin happen to mention who the witch was who cursed him?"

"Is it important?" I was good with names, but at the time Martin had shared the information, I was too busy making sure he understood my rules about privacy.

"Not necessarily, but the more information we have, the better," Joyce said.

I concentrated harder. "I think it was Isabella something."

"Fernsby?" Disgust was not a good look for Edith, or Joyce for that matter.

"Yes, Isabella Fernsby." I wiggled my finger, then listened to Joyce repeat the name to Deeann.

"In case you were wondering,"—Edith leaned closer—"we're familiar with the Fernsby family. Not a friendly bunch, but thankfully they live further up the coast, and we shouldn't have to deal with them."

Until she'd said something, I hadn't realized how much I'd been worried about the curse wielding witches or that I'd been holding my breath. "That's good to know," I said after gasping some much-needed air.

Joyce held the phone away from her head again. "Deeann has family visiting for the festival, but she can do it tonight if you're available."

Even though I had no idea what 'it' was, I'd made a promise to Martin and planned to keep it. "I guess that will work."

"Tonight is fine." Joyce nodded a few times. "Uh-huh...yes...we'll see you there." She disconnected the call and shoved her phone in her skirt pocket.

Embarrassed to ask, I cleared my throat. "I know it might sound silly, but is what we're doing going to be painful or involve blood?"

"No, but you will need to meet us at the cemetery at nine this evening," Joyce said.

Why was it every time I tried to do a good deed for someone I ended up in the graveyard? "Do you think Deeann will mind if I bring Shawna and Jade with me?" If Deeann, Joyce, and Edith really were witches and going to be performing spells, there was no way I was going without my friends.

Joyce flicked her wrist. "Of course not."

"Oh, and you'll need to bring Martin with you as well," Edith said.

I wasn't sure why everyone assumed I had a speed dial to the ghostly realm and could summon spirits at will. Even if I did talk to him before tonight, I couldn't guarantee he'd show up. "I'll see what I can do."

Edith turned to Joyce. "We'll also need to clear our visit and make sure someone tells Clyde."

Clyde was getting on in age and had a tendency to sleep through most of his shift. Letting him know we'd be tromping around the cemetery was a good thing, and relieved my concern about us startling him unnecessarily, or having him call the police to report us.

"Deeann is taking care of it. All we need to do is show up."

The door opened, the bell tinkled, and three teenage girls entered the shop giggling. They must have been here before because after giving Edith and Joyce a quick greeting, they headed for the display case Martin had been perusing earlier.

"Okay, then. I guess I'll see you later." I started to leave but didn't make it far before Edith rushed around me to hold the door open.

"Rylee, just remember things are not always as they appear. Sometimes what you see can be deceiving."

She'd done the same thing at the end of my previous visit, and her words of advice were no less cryptic than they were the last time. "What does that mean?"

"You'll figure it out." With a shrug and a smile, she closed the door behind me.

CHAPTER FIFTEEN

The main gate leading into the By the Bay cemetery was unlocked, so I drove my car through the entrance and parked next to the only other two vehicles in the lot. Unlike my friends, who were excited about our meeting with Deeann, Joyce, and Edith, I wasn't thrilled about returning to the cemetery. Even if we did have permission to be there.

Judging by the permanent scowl Martin made for the entire drive, I didn't think he was happy about going either. He'd gone back to wearing his pirate outfit, which made his annoyance appear even more intimidating.

My concern about finding him after the visit with Edith and Joyce hadn't lasted long. He'd been waiting for me outside the Classic Broom. It had taken me the entire walk back to my family's shop to convince him that no one planned to send him to the other side and that his presence was required to find Pete. He'd finally agreed when I'd pointed out that Pete might be upset to be greeted by a group of strangers and vanish again.

I was out of my realm when it came to summoning a cursed spirit. What if something went wrong or their plan backfired? Even though Joyce and Edith seemed confident

129

in Deeann's abilities, I was still worried.

As soon as I told Shawna and Jade where we were going, I'd invoked our non-sharing rule to ensure they didn't tell anyone else about what we were doing. Even though I was grateful for Bryce's help, I didn't think Joyce's invitation to bring friends included the spoofers.

If Grams hadn't already been scheduled to meet with Nadine to discuss last-minute plans for the festival tomorrow, I would have asked her to come with us. Bringing her along would have been better than her showing up with Mattie, and possibly Josh, in the middle of whatever magical thing Deeann was doing.

So far, my attempts to avoid Josh and his misguided notion that we were meant to be together, had been fairly successful. And until he left to go back home in two days, I planned to keep it that way.

"Rylee, was there a dress code you forgot to mention?" Jade asked when she got out of the vehicle and got a look at what the Haverston sisters were wearing.

I'd never seen Joyce and Edith dressed in any kind of outfit that didn't include a long skirt. It was strange to see them in dark jeans and matching black jackets as if they were part of a covert mission. They'd secured their long hair in a single braid down the center of their backs. Dark smudges on their pale cheeks were the only thing they lacked to blend into their surroundings.

"Not that I'm aware of." It was too late to go home and change out of the jeans and long-sleeved shirts we were all wearing.

"Good evening, ladies," Edith pulled her hands out of her jacket pockets as she approached us. "I'm so glad you could make it."

Telling her I was happy to be here would be fabricating the truth. I was struggling with the urge to race back to the safety of my car and offered her a forced smile before asking, "Where's Deeann?" I was curious to meet the woman who was supposedly going to solve my finding

Pete dilemma.

"She's already inside waiting for us." Joyce motioned toward the entrance on the other side of the lot.

"Is Martin here?" Edith glanced around as if trying to sense his presence.

"He's…" I caught a glimpse of him frowning from his seat in the back of my car. With a shake of my head, I walked over and knocked on the window. "Martin, aren't you coming?" I was tempted to tell him I'd send him to the other side myself if he didn't get out of the car.

"Aye," he grunted, then slid through the closed door to stand next to me.

The chill radiating from him, no doubt a result of his mood, was a lot colder than normal.

"Is there a problem?" Joyce asked when I rubbed my arms and scooted a step to the right.

Nothing a smack across the back of his head wouldn't cure, provided I could actually touch the infuriating ghost. "Nope, we're good."

"Wonderful, then let's get going." Joyce reached inside the back of her car, pulled out a flashlight, and a bag with her shop's logo embossed in the plastic, then headed for a side gate leading into the graveyard.

Shawna leaned in close to me and asked, "What do you think is in the bag?"

My imagination went crazy, filling with images of daggers, magical wands, and small containers used for body parts. "Not sure I want to know," I whispered back.

"And neither do you." Jade grabbed the sleeve of Shawna's jacket when it looked like she might hurry to catch up with Joyce and ask her.

Once we were all inside the cemetery, Joyce latched the gate behind us and flicked on her light. Finding my way around the place at night was a struggle, so I happily let Joyce and Edith lead the way.

"We're meeting Deeann near Martin's crypt." Edith glanced over her shoulder.

After hearing her mention his faux resting place, I'd expected to receive another blast of chilled air from Martin. Instead, he silently paced behind the sisters, staying a couple of feet in front of me. Miniature lights spaced evenly on the ground provided additional lighting for the graveled walkways. The sisters used the one that wound its way between several rows of gravestones before turning onto a bricked path leading toward the area filled with mausoleums.

It didn't take us long to reach the crypt the town had built in his honor. The concrete building had two overhead spotlights mounted on each corner near the roof. The two in front were aimed at Martin's name chiseled above the entrance. The door was chained and had a heavy padlock securing the links.

"There you are." A short woman, maybe an inch over five feet, peeked around the side of the building.

Her dark hair was cut short and brushed against her neck below her ears, the straight strands curled on the ends to accentuate her rounded cheeks. She was dressed similarly to Joyce and Edith.

Shawna and Jade took one look at the woman's outfit and rolled their eyes at me. "I swear I didn't know."

"Didn't know what?" Edith asked.

"Nothing," Shawna, Jade, and I said at the same time, our voices sounding as if we'd practiced saying the word together for hours.

"I'm Rylee, and you must be Deeann." I held out my hand, hoping introductions would distract Edith from asking any more questions. "And these are my friends, Shawna and Jade." I pointed to each of them in turn.

"It's nice to meet you." She flashed us a cheery smile.

"You're not at all what I'd expected," Shawna said. "You know, for someone who summons the dead."

"Oh, geez," Jade groaned, covering her face with her hands as she shook her head.

Deanna didn't seem to take offense. "What were you

expecting?"

"I don't know, maybe more Goth, a tattoo or two."

Deeann giggled. "What, no pointy black hat?"

Shawna laughed. "Now that you mention it."

"To be honest, I only speak to spirits, I don't actually see them, not like Rylee can." It's the magic that summons them. How I dress is optional," Deeann said.

"That totally makes sense." Shawna tapped her chin. "So, if you wanted to dance around naked…"

"I could." She patted her wide hips. "But I wouldn't want to risk giving poor Clyde a heart attack if he caught me."

"That be too bad," Martin said. "I rather liked yer friend's idea."

As much as I enjoyed the playful banter, Martin's grins usually led to mischief and the cemetery was the last place I wanted him to cause trouble. "So, how does this work? What do we have to do to find Pete?"

"Oh, before we get started…" Joyce held out the bag she'd been carrying to Deeann.

As soon as Deeann gripped it around the middle, Shawna eased forward. I was curious to see the contents myself, but not anxious enough to get any closer.

Deeann peeled back the plastic edges, revealing the end of a rectangular box with the word "OUIJA" printed in caps and black letters along the cream-colored edge. "This is perfect, thank you."

The familiar box reminded me of a late-night horror show I'd once seen, one that didn't end well for the game participants. "Please tell me you're not planning to use that game to help us find Pete."

"Oh, heavens no." Deeann's snort sounded like an admonishing giggle. "These things don't really work." She slipped the box back into the bag before setting it on the ground near the front of the crypt. "I got this for my daughter and her friends. They're having a slumber party for her birthday after the festival tomorrow."

I gave the box another skeptical glance remembering my last birthday present and how well that had turned out for me. I secretly envied Deeann's daughter for having a parent who gave her safe gifts, not the kind that caused life-changing paranormal experiences.

"Let's get started." Deeann waved us toward the back of the building. Shiny stones glowing an iridescent blue had been placed on the ground a foot apart and formed a three-quarter circle large enough for four people to stand next to each other. The remainder of the beautiful rocks sat off to the side in an open plastic container.

Joyce and Edith acted as if they knew what to expect and moved to the opposite side of the semi-circle.

While Martin kept his distance, Jade huddled on one side of me, Shawna on the other.

"Do you really think this is going to work?" I asked Deeann.

"What I do doesn't usually involve curses. Breaking another witch's spell can be difficult, and I can't guarantee the results." She walked over and picked up the container. "From what Joyce told me, I think we're dealing with simple binding magic."

Martin harrumphed and crossed his arms. "T'was nothing simple about bein' trapped wit' me saber all them years."

"Maybe you should have thought of that before you tried to steal from a witch," I snapped. Talking about magic, combined with being stuck in the cemetery in the middle of the night, was wearing on my patience. It was also bringing out my persnickety side.

Deeann's dark eyes sparkled with amusement. "I guess I don't need to ask if Martin is here."

"He is," I said.

"Good, then let's get started." She pointed at the rocks on the ground. "I need you and Martin to stand in the middle of the circle. Once you're inside, I'll close it off with the rest of the stones."

"I nah be goin' anywhere nigh whatever that be." Martin stomped his foot, his anger turning the air around me frigid.

Shawna and Jade must have felt it too because they moved closer to Joyce and Edith.

I pulled my jacket tighter across my chest. "Martin, you need to calm down."

"Rylee, is there a problem?" Deeann asked.

"Martin refuses to go in the circle because he thinks you'll send him to the other side." I didn't want to go in either. Not because I thought I'd end up in another world inhabited by spirits. I was more afraid to find out what other magic the seeker had stuck me with. What if the spell backfired and I ended up with a dozen or so ghosts following me around?

"My skills are limited to summoning, but if he'd rather not try to find Pete, I'll understand." Deeann walked over to the circle, then took her time reaching for the nearest stone.

She definitely had the motherly persuasive skills honed to perfection. It only took Martin a few seconds of pondering what she'd said to realize this was his last chance to find his friend.

"Tell her I changed me mind," he growled.

"Martin says he'll do it." The chill subsided, and I loosened the grip on my coat.

"Before I step inside, can you tell me why you need both of us?" I could understand why she might need Martin. He had close ties to Pete.

"Since we don't have anything that belonged to Pete, I believe your spirit seeking ability and your connection to Martin will help us find him," Deeann said.

Jade squeezed my arm. "Are you sure *you* want to do this?"

Not really, but Spencer's kept their promises no matter what. I also had Max to think about. What if whoever killed Jake was determined to make sure my uncle got blamed for it? What else would they be willing to do? They'd already killed once. Would they do it again?

If finding Pete worked and Martin kept his part of our deal, then his ghostly abilities would come in handy. "I have to try." I turned to Martin. "Come on, let's get this over with."

After a curt nod, he reluctantly followed me into the circle.

"I guess we're ready. Is there anything else we need to do?" I hoped the sisters had been telling the truth about no pain or blood being required for the ceremony.

"No, but it is important that you don't leave the circle until I'm finished," Deeann said.

That sounded a little more ominous than I'd have liked, and was glad it hadn't caused Martin to vanish.

"How long will it take?" I asked Deeann as she placed the remaining stones on the ground.

"If the spell works the way I hope it will, then it shouldn't take more than a few minutes."

"Wow, that's pretty fast," Shawna said.

"It usually takes longer if I have to kill a chicken." Deeann winked, then quickly added, "Just kidding." She set the now empty container off to the side again. "No animals are ever harmed during the process."

I joined my friends in a round of laughter. Even Martin couldn't hold back a smirk. "It ain't often ye meet a witch wit' a sense of humor."

Before I could ask him how many witches he'd actually met, Deeann held up her hands and started chanting. The air around me crackled with electricity and enveloped me in a blanket of warmth. It wasn't painful, but it lifted the ends of my hair as if I'd been caught in an upward breeze. I thought about Martin's comment, the one where he referred to me as a beacon, and worried that I'd made the wrong decision.

The natural glow of the rocks when I'd first seen them was nothing compared to the way they were shimmering now. Even Martin was covered in a thick haze of blue. The pressure in my chest tightened, and it was hard not to compare what had happened during my previous spirit seeker experience with the current situation. All it would take was a single tendril to emerge from one of the stones and spiral in my direction for me to break my promise about staying in the circle.

The sound of barking in the distance refocused my fear. Had Deeann's chanting missed its mark entirely and attracted a hound, or possibly more, from a realm filled with fire and brimstone?

I glanced outside the circle. Deeann's eyes were closed, and she continued to chant as if she were in a trance. Jade and Shawna stared at the wall of blue with awestruck expressions on their faces. Joyce and Edith stood next to them, apparently just as impressed with the magical display.

I turned back toward Martin, expecting him to be as panicked as I was. Instead, his scowl had vanished, replaced by a beaming smile. "Did you hear that?"

"I did indeed, Lass."

"Aren't you afraid?" I gave him my back and stared at the fading wall of blue, nervously waiting for the beast I'd heard to pounce on me any second.

"Nah, why would I be?" he asked, then tilted his head in the direction from which the barking continued to get louder.

Deeann stopped chanting and opened her eyes. "Rylee, did it work? I don't hear any voices. Can you see Pete?"

"No Pete, but a whole lot of…" A flash of dark tan sailed past me right into Martin's chest. I took a step back and almost tripped over a rock.

The massive beast with large fangs and claws I'd expected turned out to be a large dog with gangly legs, long floppy ears, and a leather patch over one eye. He wagged his tail so fast I was sure I'd felt a breeze, then licked the side of Martin's face with the longest ghostly tongue I'd ever seen.

"I be missing you too, lad." Martin wrapped his arms around the lovable beast.

"What's happening?" Jade asked as she moved closer to the outside of the circle with Shawna, Joyce, and Edith doing the same.

I gave my friends a disbelieving smile. "It's funny how Martin neglected to mention his best mate is a dog." Or maybe he'd been afraid I wouldn't help him if he'd told me the truth.

"A dog, really?" Shawna asked. "I wish we could see him. What does he look like?"

Everyone in the group stared at me expectantly, a reminder that I was the only one who could see Pete and Martin. "He looks like a *dog*." I wasn't an expert on pets and couldn't tell them if Pete was a specific breed or an overly friendly mutt.

"Yeah, that narrows it down." Jade chuckled.

I would have asked Martin about Pete's lineage, but the two of them were busy getting reacquainted, and I hated to interrupt. "Okay, a big light brown dog with long legs."

"Not much better," Shawna said.

"Fine, next time we're in front of a computer, I'll find a picture for you."

"I'm just glad we were right about your magic." Joyce smiled at Edith, then back at me.

"Me too, otherwise things could have turned out quite differently, even badly," Deeann said.

Badly? It annoyed me that no one had said anything about things going wrong before I'd stepped into the circle.

"What were you right about?" Jade asked before I could vent my frustration out loud.

"Rylee's gift being strong," Deeann answered as she picked up each of the stones and placed them in her container.

The sisters and I had discussed my abilities on two

occasions, and sadly neither of them provided a remedy on how to get rid of it. I still wasn't convinced about the gift part, but after undergoing the ritual to summon Pete, I was more than willing to agree to the strong part.

Shawna walked over to help Deeann with the last of the stones. "Can you do your summoning thing with any spirit?"

"It depends, why?" Deeann waited for Shawna to drop the last rock into the container before snapping the lid into place.

Shawna's question was definitely a precursor to trouble and made me cringe. "The police think Rylee's uncle is responsible for Jake Durant's death. It would sure be helpful if she could talk to his spirit and find out who really killed him." She tossed an innocent smile in my direction. "Don't you think?"

I'd agree if I wasn't afraid I'd end up being stuck with the rude man's ghost for more than ten minutes. I wasn't the only one who thought disturbing Jake was a bad plan. Edith clamped a hand over her gasp. Joyce made a disapproving noise. Jade remained silent, her masked face hard to read. If I had to guess, she was weighing the benefits of agreeing with Shawna or throttling her for making an assumption before discussing it with me first.

Deeann's eyes widened, and she tightened her grip on the container. "Ooh, that is *not* a good idea."

"It's not?" I might not want to participate in a summoning ever again, but it didn't mean I wasn't curious to know why the question had upset Deeann.

"If a person wasn't pleasant in life, there's a chance they'll be even worse in death," Deeann said. "That's why I only deal with spirits who left the world naturally…when it's their scheduled time."

"But you helped Martin, and he was cursed." I shot a sidelong glance at the ghost who was petting his four-legged friend.

"The circumstances were different," Deeann said.

"You'd already broken his curse, and I believed you could do the same for Pete."

"And it turns out you were right," Joyce said. "Anyway, we should probably get going. Tomorrow will be a long day for all of us." Edith took a few steps toward the side of the crypt, then stopped to wait for Joyce and Deeann to catch up.

With all that had transpired, I'd almost forgotten about the festival.

"Long but most definitely fun." Shawna wiggled her brows, then hurried to follow.

"Come on, oh, glorious ghost whisperer." Jade smiled, then hooked her arm through mine.

Speaking of spirits, I glanced back over my shoulder. "Martin, are you coming?"

He stopped petting Pete long enough to look up and grin. "Lass, I be eternally grateful fer yer help, but me mate and me needs to go. Thank the witch fer me, will ye?" Barking and laughter was the last thing I heard as Martin and Pete faded into nothingness.

CHAPTER SIXTEEN

Grams and I had closed the shop early since all the festivities would be held in a designated area near the docks. She'd already left to help Nadine with the last-minute preparations for the fortune teller booth. Barley and I had returned to my apartment, so I could change into my costume while I waited for Jade and Shawna to arrive.

Max had sent me a text to let me know he had plenty of supplies and to tell me that a group of his friends and his employees would be busy preparing for the pirate battle the *Buccaneer's Delight* would be participating in later that day. The competition was one of my favorite events. The two boats weren't armed with real weapons, but watching grown men use water cannons to take out their opponents was always entertaining.

Feeling a little melancholy, I'd done my best to stay busy, so I wouldn't have to think about Martin's abrupt departure. Problematic situations or not, I'd gotten used to having him around. I had actually hoped he'd stick around long enough to help my friends and I find Jake's killer. I would be the first to admit I didn't know nearly enough about the rules governing ghosts. Maybe there were forces from the otherworld that beckoned him, and leaving had been out of his control.

Since there was nothing I could do to change things, I decided to focus my energies on the land of the living. I snatched Barley off the floor, then settled into a chair at the kitchen table to review the piece of paper containing my minuscule list of suspects.

After speaking with Lucas, I was convinced he wasn't the killer and had scratched a line through his name. Leaving room for notes, I'd spaced Braden, Arlene, and Amanda's names out evenly on the remainder of the sheet. If there was anyone else who should be added, I didn't know who they were or how to go about finding them. I might have narrowed down my list, but I was still no closer to figuring out who had actually wanted Jake dead and why.

I leaned back in my seat and scratched Barley behind the ears. He closed his eyes, his low purr turning into a loud rumble. "I don't suppose you could magically uncover a clue that would help me figure out who the killer is, could you?" He responded with a meow and pushed his head against my palm when I dared to stop scratching.

I didn't like encouraging my grandmother's so-called psychic predictions, and might never vocally admit reincarnation was possible. But at the moment, I wouldn't mind a visit and some otherworldly help from my great-great uncle Howard. Even if his last supposed visit had been in the form of a mouse who enjoyed eating my muffins. Unfortunately, the little critter's visits had stopped shortly after my friends and I had said our farewells to Jessica.

Not only did the rap on the door make me jump, but it also startled Barley. He dug his sharp nails into my thighs when he sprang from my lap to hide under the couch. "Ow, Barley, that hurt," I scolded as I rubbed the part of my skirt covering my legs before getting up to answer the door.

I barely had a chance to twist the handle before Shawna burst into the room. "Did you hear the latest?"

"Good morning to you too." I moved out of the way and waited for Jade to follow her inside before closing the door. "Hey, I like the new outfit." Jade rarely wore the same costume more than two years in a row. She hadn't been kidding when she'd told me about her plans to be a sexy swashbuckler. Her low-cut bodice was laced along the front, and her ruffled red skirt hit mid-thigh, a lot shorter than anything I dared to wear.

Shopping for clothes wasn't my thing, so I'd chosen to wear the bar wench costume I purchased the year before. It was nowhere near the attention-getter Jade's was, but I hoped it would be enough to catch Logan's eye.

Shawna's interests were different and leaned toward the masculine side. She'd gone with a high seas captain look. Her outfit consisted of a long burgundy vest beneath a dark brown overcoat and leather boots that reached her knees. She'd even found a fake pistol to complete the ensemble. "What does Nate think about your costume?"

"He hasn't seen it yet." Shawna rocked back and forth on her feet, then waved the newspaper she was carrying in my face. "Aren't you even the slightest bit interested to hear what I found out?"

Her persistence most likely meant the news was something I wouldn't be happy to hear about. And after my adventure in the cemetery the night before, I was too exhausted to share her enthusiasm. "Not if it has anything to do with my horoscope."

"You might as well let her tell you; otherwise, we'll never get out of here." Jade settled into the chair next to the one I'd been occupying.

"All right, let's have it." I returned to my seat and waited for Shawna to lay the paper on the table.

The article she pointed at took up a small square space on the first page. "According to a group of teenagers attending a campfire party on the beach last night, there was a pirate ship floating in the bay."

Jade quirked a brow but didn't say anything. No doubt she'd already voiced her opinion on the subject before they'd arrived.

In our youth, we'd attended more than one of the many parties held in the cove during the spring and summer months, so I frowned and stated the obvious. "I don't suppose the article mentions how much alcohol was consumed before the so-called sighting, does it?"

"No, but don't you think it's a coincidence that a pirate ship shows up around the same time that Deeann worked her hocus pocus to summon Pete?" she asked.

"Oooh, and what if having you help with the spell somehow brought Martin's whole crew back from the briny depths?" Sarcasm laced Jade's teasing tone.

"How cool would that be?" Shawna's grin faded after I shot a glare in her direction. "Or not."

"Let's hope it was a hoax." It wouldn't be the first time someone had reported seeing a ship that wasn't there. "Because the thought of a bunch of pirate ghosts that only I can see showing up all over town and raising havoc is upsetting my stomach." Not to mention the headache I was getting from thinking about the disaster it would cause.

Shawna glanced back at the newspaper. "There aren't any pictures, so maybe you're right, maybe it was a hoax." Her disappointment outweighed her attempt to be supportive.

"Wha' did I miss?" Martin appeared in the middle of the living room with Pete sitting on the floor next to him. He'd changed back into his tourist ensemble and had even gotten a bright yellow bandanna and tied it around Pete's neck.

"Martin," I stammered and jumped to my feet. "I thought you left, you know, as in permanently."

"Martin's here?" Jade sounded more confused than I

felt. "But you said he was gone."

I tried to take a step and realized I'd caught the hem of my skirt on the heel of my boot when I'd gotten up. I braced my hand on the end of the table to keep from stumbling, then unhooked the fabric before straightening. "Well, Martin did make it sound as if he was leaving for good before he poofed out."

He wrinkled his nose. "Lass, I shall 'ave ye know I do nah *poof*. I went somewhere to spend time alone wit' Pete."

"Fair enough, so what are you doing back here?" I rested my hands on my hips. "Now that you've resolved your unfinished business, aren't you supposed to be moving on?"

He puffed out his chest. "Me business, as ye say, ain't complete."

"It's not?" I asked warily, afraid that Pete wasn't the only thing he expected me to find.

"Nah, Lass, I made ye a promise, 'n I intend to keep it." As soon as Martin straightened and took his hand off Pete's head, the dog began sniffing along the bottom edge of the sofa.

Barley was still hiding underneath. Was it possible the spirit hound could smell him?

"What did he say?" Jade asked.

I smiled at my friends. "He still wants to help us find Jake's killer."

CHAPTER SEVENTEEN

Martin and Pete's surprise visit to my apartment had delayed Shawna, Jade, and my departure to the festival, but not by much. We arrived twenty minutes before the grounds officially opened. People were already milling around. Although a large number of them wore some type of pirate-related costume, not everyone who attended the festival felt inclined to dress the part.

The town had devised all kinds of activities for the attending pirate enthusiasts. The most popular event was the swordplay area, designed for anyone who wanted to show off their blade-wielding abilities. For the price of a ticket, anyone could select the sword of their choice and battle it out with whomever they wanted.

Another area had been cordoned off for a carnival that specifically catered to children. Besides the handful of rides and game booths, there was also face painting and treasure hunts.

A costume contest had been scheduled for later in the day, one which Shawna and Jade had entered. Most of the food booths were already serving. Several of them, including the one for the cantina where Shawna worked, had people forming lines. Brant was behind the counter wearing a chef's apron with his business logo and was busy taking orders. He paused long enough to smile and wave as we walked by.

We were halfway through the food court when I felt Martin's chill and knew he was keeping his promise to meet us here. He appeared on my right with Pete strolling along beside him. "Lass." He greeted me with a tip of his head. "I be ready to start whenever ye be."

Since walking with Shawna and Jade made talking to Martin much easier, I didn't bother retrieving the cell out of my purse. "Start?" I asked after giving him a quick sidelong glance. The way he was checking out the people and booths, I wondered if he'd meant the festivities.

"Aye, our search fer the bloke who used me saber to do in Jake."

In case anyone in the crowds we passed was listening, I carefully worded what I said to Shawna and Jade. "Our mutual friend would like to get started on helping Max."

"It sounds like a decent plan," Jade said. "Everyone in question should be here."

She was referring to the list I'd shown her and Shawna on the drive over. I'd also filled them in on my conversation with Lucas, and they agreed with my decision to remove his name as a suspect.

The *Sea Witch* was one of the boats participating in the battle, so Braden and Arlene were guaranteed to be present. Amanda would be here as well. The woman never missed a festival or the opportunity to point out the costumes she'd designed to potential new customers.

The conversation Martin overheard between Braden and an unknown caller was still our best clue. Actually, it was our only clue. Arlene and Amanda had been added based on speculation, not anything concrete. It didn't mean they were responsible, it only meant my friends and I hadn't found anything substantial to investigate.

"Any suggestions about how we should proceed?" Jade asked.

Shawna rubbed her hands together, excited to be involved in another one of our so-called covert missions. "Our targets might already be here. Maybe we should split up, do some reconnaissance, then meet back here in an hour."

Her idea made sense, but Shawna investigating by herself was almost as bad as letting Grams run around unsupervised. I shared a worried glance with Jade, then offered a distraction. "I promised Grams we'd check in with her as soon as we arrived."

Shawna's eyes brightened. "Is she helping Nadine?

I hesitated before saying yes. I knew the real reason behind her enthusiastic response had to do with the destination and not checking in with my grandmother. My friend was the only person I knew who lived to have her fortune read so she'd know what to expect in the upcoming year. I bet if I checked her pockets, I'd find a piece of paper with all the questions she planned to ask Nadine.

"That's awesome. Let's absolutely stop there first." She adjusted the fake pistol tucked into her wide leather belt and picked up her pace.

Martin cleared his throat. "Lass, be that nah yer new beau?"

I turned my head in his direction, expecting to see him pointing at Logan and saw Josh instead. "Very funny," I muttered through gritted teeth when he chuckled.

I'd never paid much attention to Josh or his costumes in the past. The tan and black-striped pants, along with his ruffled white shirt, looked a little snug, and I wondered if it was the same outfit he'd worn when he'd worked for my uncle.

Luckily, Josh was too busy ogling a couple of women dressed in outfits even more revealing than Jade's. Once he saw me with my friends, he'd know I wasn't working, and I'd be stuck with him following me around for the rest of the day.

"What's funny?" Jade asked.

"Josh alert." I grabbed Shawna's and Jade's sleeves and tugged them toward the closed flap leading into the tent behind Nadine's ticket collecting booth, which I assumed one of her employees would be arriving soon to manage.

Jade wasn't eager to have Josh stalking us all day, either. "Do you think he saw us?" she asked after stopping in the middle of the waiting area, a rectangular shaped room with two metal folding chairs sitting along the fabric walls on both sides of the entrance.

"I don't know." I turned to ask Martin if he'd check to see if Josh was still hanging around outside and couldn't find him anywhere. "He has got to be the most frustrating ghost I've ever met."

"Martin's back?" Grams asked as she entered from the room where Nadine did her readings and lowered the heavy cloth flap behind her.

Instead of a pirate costume, my grandmother wore a medium-sleeved red blouse beneath a gold vest and a long black skirt covered with miniature gold stars and moons. Wisps of silver-streaked hair peeked out along the edges of a black scarf tied in a knot and covering her ear on the right side of her head. Clipped to her other ear was a hoop style earring, at least two inches in diameter.

If she was dressed like a fortune teller, it meant she'd be helping Nadine most of the day. It also meant I had one less person to worry about getting into trouble.

"He was, but he pulled another one of his disappearing acts," I said.

"Hey, Grams," Shawna greeted my grandmother with a hug. "Where's Nadine?"

"She's finishing up inside." Grams hitched a thumb over her shoulder. "I'm sure she won't mind if you go in."

Shawna grabbed the edge of the material and stopped. "Now that we're here, you should definitely have Nadine read your future."

Jade wiggled her brows and smiled. "Maybe she can

give you some good relationship advice."

Shawna's giggle earned her the same glare I'd narrowed at Jade. "Or maybe she can tell me if I need new best friends."

"Actually, I thought she might be able to help with your sleuthing problem," Shawna said.

"Since Max is the suspect, wouldn't it be smarter to have her take a look at his future instead of mine?" I didn't need to be a psychic to know the determined flicker in her eyes meant she wasn't ready to give up.

"Aren't you curious to find out about Logan?" Shawna asked.

"What about him?" The question sounded more defensive than I'd intended.

"Wouldn't you like to know if he's the *one*?" Jade asked.

It was never a good thing when she decided to side with Shawna, especially if I was their intended target. So far, Grams hadn't chimed in, which was out of character for her. Her abstinence might have been based on guilt about her role in my current Josh predicament. Guilt that would hopefully keep her from interfering until after his Monday departure.

In the meantime, I wasn't going to make it easy for my friends. "Of course, I would, but sometimes it's better to be surprised."

Jade held up her hand. "But you hate surprises."

"I do, but in this case, I'm okay with making an exception." I tucked my arms across my chest and refused to budge.

"If you aren't going to get a reading, at least come inside and listen to mine." Shawna draped her arm across the back of my shoulder. "Please." Her begging turned into a whine. A whine I knew would get much worse if she didn't get her way. When Jade wrapped her arm around me from the other side and pouted, I finally relented.

Grams grinned, holding the flap open as Shawna and Jade pulled me inside.

"Ladies, I've been expecting you." Nadine's blue eyes twinkled as she looked up from setting a crystal ball in the center of a round table. She was dressed in an outfit similar to Grams's; only her color-coordinated skirt and blouse were done in shades of blue and yellow. Her long dark hair had been pulled to one side, the braid hanging in front of her shoulder.

"Rylee, have you finally decided to get a reading?" Nadine smoothed the wrinkles out of the red cloth with black and gold magical symbols sewn into the fabric near the hem that was draped over the table.

"No, I'm only here to show support." I left out the part that it wasn't voluntary, that I'd been coerced. I strolled toward the long wooden table covered with lit candles and pirate paraphernalia she had sitting off to one side. Among the objects was a saber that looked a lot like Martin's. Maybe it had belonged to someone in his crew. "Is this real?" The blade was more than likely curse free, but I refrained from touching it anyway.

"You'd be surprised how many people ask me that same question." Nadine walked over to stand next to me. "It's actually a replica."

"A pretty good imitation by the looks of it," Shawna said after she and Jade joined us. "Where did you get it?"

"Hildie over at the Booty Bazaar sells them," Nadine said.

"Can I see?" Grams squeezed between Nadine and me, then tapped the blade.

"Grams," I warned when her fingertips skimmed the hilt as if she was planning to pick up the blade. The last thing I needed was my grandmother demonstrating her scary sword-swinging abilities in a confined space.

She dismissed me with a snort. "It could almost be a twin to the one Maxwell has, or I should say had, since Roy confiscated it after they found it stuck in Jake."

Things are not always as they appear. Sometimes what you see can be deceiving. I wasn't sure why Edith's parting words picked that moment to pop into my head, but it was the clue I needed to uncover the killer's identity and possibly solve the murder.

***

By the time I'd used a fabricated excuse to convince Jade and Shawna we needed to leave, people were lining up to see Nadine. Explaining that I needed to find Martin without bringing up his name had been a bit of a challenge. Not that finding the ghost was going to be any easier.

Thankfully, Jade had caught on right away and helped me usher Shawna from the tent. If Grams hadn't already promised to greet and sell tickets for Nadine, I'm sure she would have insisted she go with us.

"I still don't understand why I couldn't get my reading from Nadine first." Luckily, Shawna's scowl wasn't accompanied by a more noticeable tantrum. She'd waited to voice her concern until after we'd walked behind the tent and away from any people.

After peeking around the corner to make sure Josh wasn't lurking nearby and hadn't seen us, I took a deep breath to gather my thoughts and keep from rambling. "I might have discovered a clue to Jake's murder, and I didn't want to discuss it in front of Nadine."

"Well, in that case." Shawna's irritation immediately evaporated into a beaming smile. "Please share."

I reached into my purse for my cell. "I need to make a quick call first." I thumbed the screen and hit the autodial. "Hey, Uncle Max," I said as soon as he answered.

"Rylee, is everything okay?" Concern deepened his voice.

"Everything's fine. I know you're busy, but I have a question." Jade and Shawna moved a little closer, seeming to be a lot more interested to hear what I had to say.

"Sure, what did you need to know?"

"Do you remember the day Grams found your saber, and you mentioned it might be haunted because of all the strange places it kept turning up?" Though I already knew his assumption was correct, that Martin was the culprit, it wasn't my reason for asking.

"Yes, why?" His curiosity piqued and reminded me a lot of my father whenever anyone mentioned the paranormal.

"Is there anyone besides the three of us who might have known?"

"My employees, for sure. Chloe and Lucas found it a couple of times. We all liked to joke about it." He sounded amused as if recalling some of their past conversations.

"Can you think of anyone else who might have known?"

"Let me think." I imagined him scratching his beard during the brief pause. "Oh, and Hildie. As a matter of fact, she stopped by the boat and offered to buy it back from me."

"Really?"

"Yes. She seemed awfully upset when I told her no," Max said.

"When was this?" I asked.

"I'd say a week or so ago. Not long after I'd had it authenticated."

My mind whirled with the new information, but I still needed to confirm a few more facts from other sources.

"Does this have something to do with Jake's murder?" he asked.

"I don't know, but I've got to go. Good luck this afternoon." I disconnected the call before he could ask any more questions.

As soon as I slipped the phone back into my purse, I glanced around to make sure we were still alone before sharing my speculations with Jade and Shawna. "Do you remember me telling you what Edith said before I left the Classic Broom?"

"You mean about things not being what they appear?" Jade asked.

"Yes." I nodded. "And seeing the saber replica made me wonder if it had something to do with Jake's death." Before my friend's bewildered expressions turned into questions, I continued with the rest of my theory. "Ever since the day we found him, I've been trying to figure out who would want Max to take the blame. What if it wasn't about getting revenge, but acquiring something he owned?"

"Do you think the murder had something to do with Martin's saber?" Jade asked.

"Suppose someone already knew the sword belonged to Martin and was worth a lot of money." I bit my lower lip. "And what if that someone tried to buy it from Max, and he refused?"

Jade snapped her fingers. "Then that someone might decide to steal it by replacing it with a replica."

"And maybe Jake found out and tried to stop them, or he was somehow involved," Shawna said.

"Did Max happen to give you the name of this someone we're speculating about?" Jade asked.

After hearing about Jake's unethical business dealings, I had a hard time believing his death was an accident. His shady practices were more than likely responsible for his death.

"He said Hildie wanted to buy the saber back, but that doesn't mean she's the killer. It only means she's a suspect." I wasn't ready to accuse her without further proof. "It is possible that someone who purchased one of her replicas is responsible." It would have to be someone who knew the value of the saber and also knew my uncle and Jake.

"The list would have to be short." Shawna furrowed her brow. "I can't imagine Hildie going around telling a lot of people what the saber was worth, not if she wanted to get her hands on it."

"I agree," Jade said.

"I do too, which is why I need Martin's help," I said.

"I don't get it," Shawna said. "What can Martin do to prove your theory?"

"Aye, I be interested to hear yer explanation meself." I squealed and jumped at the same time. I'd been so preoccupied with our conversation I hadn't noticed the drop in temperature that preceded Martin's appearance.

My friends did their best to hide their amusement, Jade by pressing her lips together and Shawna by clamping a hand over her mouth.

"What happened to you? Why didn't you come inside with us?" I asked.

He stuck out his chest. "'tis a place of magic, 'n I 'ave had me fill of witches."

"Nadine is not a witch, she only reads palms and consults her crystal ball." Though I strived for patience, I was ready for him to get over his witch phobia.

"Wha' be the purpose of this ball ye speak of?"

"Supposedly,"— I glanced at Shawna—"some people like to know what to expect in their future."

"Ye mean like the printed words of wisdom yer friend gets from that thin' ye call a newspaper?" he asked.

"Yes, something like that." I sidestepped to avoid the swish of Pete's tail. He'd been happily sniffing the ground since their arrival.

"I also thought it best to waylay Josh." His grin widened. "We cannot continue our search if ye persist in duckin' inside tents to avoid 'im."

I slapped my hands on my hips. "What did you do?" I asked, hoping that whatever he'd done to Josh hadn't drawn a lot of attention.

"Do nah worry, Lass. He had an accident wit' his drink 'n scurried off to a restroom to take care of it."

"Care to share?" Jade glanced from me to the spot where Martin was standing.

"Apparently, Josh had a minor mishap with his drink

and will be in the bathroom for a little while."

"One problem temporarily solved, so what do we do next?" Shawna asked.

"We send our ghostly friend to do some reconnaissance." I turned to Martin. "Do you remember telling me about the mark you made on your saber below the hilt?"

"I remember, but I do nah understand why 'tis important," Martin said.

"Because if my assumption is correct." And I was pretty sure it was. "Then the saber used to dispense with Jake was a fake."

"Oooh, and you want Martin to sneak into the police evidence room to see if you're right." Shawna's gaze sparkled with a conspiratorial gleam.

"Yes." I glanced at Martin. "If you wouldn't mind."

Sometimes his grins were hard to read. I couldn't tell if he was happy to be helping or imagining what kind of mischief he could cause along the way.

"Ye found Pete." He patted his leg, silently commanding the dog to sit on the ground next to him. "I be glad to repay the debt."

"Let's say the saber is a duplicate, and we're fairly certain you know who is the killer or at least involved." Jade kept an eye on the people passing by the opening between the tents while she talked. "How do we go about proving it? Because if you're right, we'll need to tell Logan and Roy."

I rubbed my forehead and sighed. I hadn't given that part of the plan much thought. "Yeah, and I'm pretty sure they aren't going to believe us if we tell them we had some ghostly intervention."

"But they'd have to believe us if we found Martin's saber," Shawna said.

"Yes, they would." Feeling like we were finally making headway, I straightened my shoulders and spoke to Martin. "If the saber is a fake, can you go to the Booty Bazaar and see if the real one is stashed there?"

"'Twould be me pleasure." I didn't get a chance to remind him to behave himself. One second he was lovingly scratching Pete's head, and the next they were both gone.

"So, is Martin going to be our spy?" Jade asked.

I shook my head. "He is, and he already left."

"Do you think it'll take him long because I'm getting hungry?" Shawna placed a hand over her stomach.

The smells from the food court had wafted in our direction. One of my favorite reasons for attending the festival was the variety of delicious meals being offered, most of which were served using a pirate theme. I had quite a collection of pewter beer mugs stamped with commemorative logos and the date of the event on a shelf in my office. "Now that you mention it, I wouldn't mind grabbing something to eat while we wait."

Shawna took the lead. "If we stop by the booth for the Cantina, we can use my employee discount."

Until I had absolute proof that Hildie was the killer, had committed the crime alone, and didn't have a partner, I wasn't ready to cross anyone else off my list. Having lunch at Brant's place provided us with a central location and the ability to keep a lookout for the remaining suspects.

CHAPTER EIGHTEEN

"Any sign of Martin yet?" Jade got up from the picnic-style table where we had eaten our lunch and tossed her empty paper plate in a nearby trashcan.

"Not yet," I said as Shawna and I did the same. The pirate ship battle was scheduled to start soon, and we'd decided to head over to the dock so we could find a good place to watch.

So far, I'd seen Amanda strolling around with a couple of her friends, but no sign of Hildie, Braden, or Arlene. Though with Jake gone, there was a good chance Arlene would be helping Braden prep their team on the *Sea Witch*. She wasn't the type to get her outfit wet, but she wouldn't have a problem standing on the sidelines and giving orders.

"We need to keep an eye out for Nate." Shawna anxiously glanced around as we walked. "He sent me a text that said he was coming with Bryce and Myra and would meet us down near the docks."

"Good, then we can find out if they're planning to enter the costume contest with us," Jade said.

The festival was an annual event, and as much as I wanted to solve Jake's murder and help Martin and Pete on their way to the afterlife, I didn't want to ruin my friends' fun. I already felt guilty about Shawna not getting her reading. I didn't want to keep them from participating in the contest.

"Are you going to change your mind about entering?" Shawna's gaze lit with determination.

"Not a chance, but I will be standing on the sidelines cheering for you." If Martin came back with the answer I expected, then I'd also be keeping an eye out for Hildie and my other suspects.

We'd nearly reached the dock when we met Elliott standing off to the side, monitoring the crowds. "Hey guys, are you going to watch the show, or are you helping this year?"

"Watching." Getting drenched wasn't my idea of fun and hadn't been since I was a teenager.

"I like the outfit." I gave his costume a quick glance, my gaze lingering on the hat he'd purchased from my family's shop, the one he bought for his nephew.

Blotches of red instantly appeared on his cheeks. "Thanks."

"Are you working today, or are you off duty?" Jade asked.

Elliott hooked his thumbs in his wide leather belt. "Working, but Roy, I mean the sheriff, gave us the okay to dress up."

The information wasn't anything I didn't already know. Roy had given his staff the option for years, mostly because he liked to participate himself. "And where is Roy?" I asked, hoping Logan would be with his uncle.

"I'm not sure, but if it's important, I can call him for you." He slipped his hand in his pocket.

"No. That's not necessary. I was only curious, but thanks." I urged my friends to start walking again.

"See you later," Shawna called to Elliott over her shoulder.

Crowds were gathering by the time we arrived at the

dock and found a spot near the water's edge where we had a good view of the boats. The *Buccaneer's Delight* was positioned on our right, the *Sea Witch* on the left.

"Hey, isn't that Logan on the deck of the *Delight?*" Jade pointed toward the cannon mounted on the far end of the railing. "He makes a pretty hot pirate, don't you think?" She nudged me with her shoulder.

Logan made any outfit look good, but seeing him dressed like a pirate had me speechless and drooling. Brown stubble framed his chin, and he'd turned a black scarf into a cap on his head. The vee of his matching shirt was loosely laced across the middle. Instead of a belt, he had a burgundy sash wrapped around his waist and tied above his left hip. Tight-fitting pants and tall leather boots completed his ensemble.

"Seems like a conflict of interest for him to be supporting Max since he's a suspect in his murder investigation," Shawna said.

It wasn't uncommon for Max to grab volunteers to help operate the cannons. He usually ended up turning people away. Roy was a regular participant, but Logan wasn't. As strict as the detective was about following the rules, I had to agree that it was strange to see him on my uncle's team. I would be annoyed if I found out it was an undercover tactic to do more investigating.

Once I was finally able to stop staring, I noticed Roy was also on deck and standing to the right of Max. Whatever they were chatting about brought on an occasional laugh from both men. Lucas, Chloe, and one of her friends were also part of the group. They were each standing next to a cannon.

I glanced over at the *Sea Witch* to check out the competition. Surprisingly, Arlene was there giving last-minute instructions to her team, but there wasn't any sign of Braden. She didn't look happy to be filling in, and I could almost imagine what she was going to say to him when he finally showed up.

In the few years Braden had lived here, he'd never missed this event. I thought about the conversation Martin had mentioned. I was still leaning toward Hildie being the killer because the clues pointed in her direction. But what if I was wrong? What if Braden was the one who'd switched out the saber and committed the murder? And if he was responsible, then what was his motive?

My pondering was brought to a halt by the appearance of a small motorized boat operated by the upcoming battle's officiating referee, who was delivering Braden to the *Sea Witch*. Both men were dressed as pirates, but the man accompanying Braden wore a black and white striped vest over his costume.

After being helped aboard the boat and a short heated exchange of words with Arlene, Braden gave the referee a signal that they were ready to start.

"It won't be long now." Shawna gripped the top bar of the metal guard railing.

"Max has a pretty solid team. There's a good chance he could win it this year." Jade smiled as she moved to stand on the other side of Shawna.

The object of the competition was to see which team stayed the driest the longest. Being able to hit an opponent while dodging an incoming blast of water required some skill. I'd never been any good at it, but it was fun watching others try.

Once the referee waved his flag, the water started to flow, and I joined my friends in supporting Max's crew. I'd gotten so caught up in the moment that I'd forgotten all about Martin's trip to the police station. When he appeared out of nowhere, my squeal was swallowed by the cheering and booing coming from the surrounding crowd.

He moved aside, so Pete could stand on his hind legs with his paws planted on the lower bar of the railing. "That looks like a lot of fun. Maybe I should…"

I glared in his direction. "Don't even think about it?" I wanted to ask him what he'd discovered but decided to wait for the battle to end.

It wasn't long before the referee was blowing his whistle and waving his flag, signaling an end to the competition, and announcing my uncle's team as the winners. I was impressed to see Logan had made it through the onslaught without getting soaked. Of course, that changed when Max encouraged everyone to join in a congratulatory group hug.

"He's back," I said to Shawna and Jade as soon as the crowd began to disperse.

"Great, what did he find out?" Shawna turned and leaned with her back against the railing.

I looked to Martin for an answer.

"I be thinkin' ye be part witch." He grinned.

"A witch, why?" I almost didn't ask, too afraid he'd discovered another ability I didn't want.

"Yer prediction was correct, the saber was nah mine."

It was a good thing I was reserved in my reactions and not big on gloating; otherwise, I'd be jumping up and down. Instead of doing a rendition of a happy dance, I turned to Shawna and Jade. "I was right about the switch."

"Awesome, so what did he find out about the second part of your request?" Jade's blue gaze shifted to the area where Martin was standing.

He understood her request without me having to translate. "I went to the shop 'n searched everywhere, but me blade was nah thar, either."

"Well, that's too bad." It's not like I expected Hildie, if she was the killer, to be bold enough to display the blade in plain sight, but I was hoping she might still have it in her possession.

"I take it he didn't have any luck?" Shawna asked.

"No," I groaned, then as an afterthought, asked, "You didn't happen to see Hildie while you were searching, did you?"

"Nah, the place was closed, 'n thar be no one inside," Martin said.

I answered the inquiring raise of Jade's brow with a shake of my head.

"If the wench's whereabouts are important, Pete and I might be able to find her fer ye."

The dog was sitting on the ground next to Martin. He cocked his head to the side, lifting a floppy ear as if he understood what Martin had said.

"Can Pete really track things?" I thought about the day at my apartment when he was sniffing along the sofa. I hadn't given it much thought before but was curious to know if a ghost's senses actually worked after their deaths.

Martin cupped his hand next to his mouth and spoke softly. "Nah, his sniffer does nah work. Nah that it 'twas much better when he was alive. I jus' let 'im believe he be a great tracker, so I do nah hurt his feelin's."

I didn't think Martin would appreciate hearing that his thoughtfulness towards the animal was adorable, so I kept the thought to myself. "If that's true, then how do you plan to find Hildie?" As far as I knew, I was the only person in the area that sent out signals that attracted spirits.

"I thought ye might be havin' another one of yer brilliant ideas." I might have believed Martin was mocking me if he hadn't sounded so sincere.

"Finding her isn't going to do us any good if she doesn't have the saber with her," I said.

"Surely with all the publicity surrounding Jake's death, she wouldn't have sold it already," Jade said.

"I'll bet she found a good place to hide it." Shawna picked up a quarter-sized rock and tossed it in the water, then watched it sink out of sight. "That's what I'd do."

Jade tugged on Shawna's sleeve when she reached for another rock. "There are days when I worry about you."

"What?" Shawna shrugged. "It's not like I would actually murder anyone. I was trying to get into the mind of the killer like the profilers on my detective shows."

I pinched the bridge of my nose, sorting through what

Shawna had said. "You know she might be onto something."

"You really think so?" Shawna gave Jade one of her I-told-you-so looks.

"Not the part about getting into someone's head, because that's too scary to think about. The part about finding a place to hide the saber definitely has some potential."

CHAPTER NINETEEN

Shawna, Jade, and I had been standing around waiting for the spoofers a lot longer than anticipated. Martin and Pete had disappeared shortly after Shawna mentioned her notion about a hiding place. I was about to suggest she give Nate a call when a melodic tune rang from inside her jacket pocket.

Shawna pulled out her cell and tapped the screen. "You've got to be kidding me." She narrowed her dark eyes at her phone as if she'd like to reach inside and throttle whoever she'd received a text from.

"Is something wrong?" Jade asked.

"Nate said they got waylaid by a paranormal sighting, and that's why they're running late."

Shawna's phone jingled again, and this time she smiled. "Aww, he sent an apology and attached some cute happy faces and heart emojis, so I suppose I shouldn't stay mad at him." She held up the phone so we could see.

Jade rolled her eyes. "Oh yeah, because getting emojis from a guy after he's made you wait for a long time makes all the difference."

Glancing past my friends, I'd noticed that Max had docked his boat. As soon as the ramp settled into place,

Roy and Logan were the first to leave. Logan held his phone to his ear as they rushed off toward the main festival area, no doubt in a hurry to handle some kind of emergency.

Shortly afterward, Max sent the rest of his team on their way. He'd no doubt stayed behind to shut down the cannons and clean up before he left.

I wasn't in the mood to run interference for the argument brewing between my friends, so I opted for having a chat with my uncle instead. I placed my hand on Jade's arm. "Can you guys give me a minute? I need to talk to Max."

I was pretty sure they wouldn't care, so I didn't bother waiting for an answer before hurrying toward the boat.

"Congratulations." I stepped onto the deck, then walked over to Max and gave him a light hug making sure I avoided coming into contact with his wet clothes.

"Not to sound smug, but the win would've been more satisfying if Jake had been around to see it."

"Believe me, I won't hold it against you. Besides,"— I poked his wet sleeve and giggled—"your team earned it."

"That we did." He snagged an empty plastic water bottle off the nearby bench, then gave me a studious look. "What are you doing here instead of enjoying the festival with your friends?"

My uncle was as perceptive as my grandmother and believed in getting straight to the point. A quality I appreciated most of the time unless I was trying to stay out of trouble. Luckily, this wasn't one of those times.

"I thought you were still a suspect in Jake's murder, so I was surprised to see Detective Prescott on your team." Max wasn't as bad as Grams when it came to matchmaking. He only dabbled now and then. Addressing Logan by his first name would have been a mistake, one my uncle wouldn't have missed.

"Didn't I tell you?" He stopped what he was doing and grinned.

"Tell me what?"

"I had an alibi for the time of the murder, and once Logan confirmed it, I was in the clear."

"Alibi?" I'd been so focused on finding the killer that I hadn't realized Max might have been doing something that involved witnesses during the time Jake met his demise.

"Yes, I was at the Shivering Timbers Saloon."

"Of course you were." I wanted to smack myself in the head for not remembering that hanging out and listening to the bands on Friday nights was his favorite pastime.

He gave me a stern look. "So if you and Grams are playing sleuth, you need to stop."

"It's a little late for…" I was proud of myself for not making any embarrassing noises when Martin and Pete appeared behind my uncle. "Lass, I found it." He waved his hands excitedly.

"Late for what?" Max's curt tone and frown drew my attention.

I wanted to hear what Martin had to say, but couldn't have the conversation in front of my uncle. I also hoped my missed chance to ask Max if Hildie mentioned whether or not she'd had a buyer for the saber wasn't going to be wasted. "I meant it's getting late, and my friends are waiting." I leaned to the side and flicked my wrist in Shawna and Jade's direction. "I should really get going." I spun and hurried across the deck before he could stop me.

"Rylee," he called after me, but I kept going.

"Talk to you later and congrats again," I shouted over my shoulder as I descended the ramp. Martin was great at taking a hint and followed after me.

Even though my friends weren't far away, I couldn't risk the handful of people I rushed past overhearing a one-sided conversation. I retrieved my phone and placed it against my ear. "Okay, let's have it. What did you find?"

"Me saber. It be on the *Sea Witch* all this time."

"Are you saying it was Braden all along, that I was wrong about it being Hildie?" Disappointed, I slumped my shoulders and slowed my pace.

"Nah, ye were right about the wench. She waited 'til the crew departed, then sneaked below deck to retrieve it," he said.

Even though I couldn't grasp why Hildie would choose Jake's boat, she couldn't have picked a more perfect hiding place. "Do you know where she is now?" I was back to hurrying again, anxious to share the news with Shawna and Jade.

"The last I saw, she be minglin' 'n chattin' with people nigh the food booths." He whistled for Pete when the dog meandered off to do some more sniffing.

"That's…" I stopped what I was about to say because I'd reached my friends at the same time Nate, Bryce, and Myra strolled up to join them.

Other than a few different accessories, the spoofer's pirate costumes were similar, and I wondered if they'd gone shopping together. It was the first time I'd seen the semblance of a smile on Myra's face. She wasn't bestowing me with her usual glare, so I decided not to ask or tease them about their wardrobe selection.

"What was the supernatural emergency?" Jade propped her hands on her hips and glared at Bryce. When it came to waiting, her tolerance level was a lot lower than Shawna's. My news about the saber and Hildie was important, but it could wait until after Jade finished dealing with her brother.

"On our way over here, we ran into Josh. He told us how his drink was magically ripped from his hand, then spilled down the front of his clothes." Bryce didn't seem intimidated by his sister in the least. Nate, on the other hand, had taken a step closer to Shawna and away from the siblings.

"He wanted us to investigate because he was convinced he was being haunted or someone was using witchcraft on him," Myra said.

I glared at Martin. "I'm pretty sure it was neither."

"I figured it was Martin since I heard he hasn't left yet." Bryce tucked his hands in his pockets and smiled. "I also heard that Pete is a dog. Is it true?"

"Yes to both, but we have bigger problems than worrying about Josh." I hated to involve the spoofers, but Martin's news couldn't wait. By now, the area in and around the festival would be packed. If I wanted to find Hildie before she escaped with the saber, I was going to need all the help I could get.

"Such as?" Jade's eager tone signaled that her rant was over.

"Finding Hildie." I took the next few minutes to share my speculations with the spoofers, then I relayed what Martin told me about her and his saber.

"When I heard about what happened to Jake, I never would have considered that angle," Bryce said.

"Me neither. I was leaning toward the spouse being the killer theory myself," Nate added with a smile aimed specifically at Shawna.

I couldn't tell if he really believed Arlene was responsible or if Nate was schmoozing to stay on my friend's good side.

"Personally, I think it was ingenious to hide the saber in a place that no one would think to look for it," Shawna stated with a proud smirk. "I wish I'd thought of it."

"Geez, really?" Jade sneered at Shawna.

I'd bet anything Shawna wasn't finished, that Jade and I would have to endure some future gloating. "Anyway, instead of standing around, we need to do something."

"Rylee's right." Bryce glanced around the group, then back at me. "How do you want to handle this?" Everyone was looking at me expectantly as if they'd taken a vote, and I'd been appointed their leader.

I pondered what he'd asked. "I think we should break up into groups of two so we can cover more ground. If you see her, call me. We don't know what she's capable of, so keep your distance." Hildie had already taken one life, and I was determined to make sure she didn't take another if she felt threatened. "Once I confirm that she has Martin saber, we'll contact Logan and Roy and let them take care of her."

"That works for me. I'll go with Nate and Jade can go with you." Shawna took Nate's hand and dragged him toward the arcade area.

Bryce followed their departure with a sullen gaze, then turned to Myra. "I guess that leaves you and me."

"Come on." Myra gave him a consoling pat on the arm, then urged him in the opposite direction.

"I think we should start near the food court. It was the last place Martin said he saw Hildie," I said.

Jade fell in step beside me. "Funny how you left that detail out when you were telling everyone else to be careful."

"I didn't say anything because we've got a secret weapon."

"Oh yeah, and what would that be?" Jade asked.

I smirked and winked at Martin. "A mischievous ghost."

CHAPTER TWENTY

After twenty fruitless minutes of searching for Hildie, I typed the word "anything" into a text on my phone and sent it to Shawna and Bryce. A few seconds later, I received a "no" from Bryce and a "not yet" from Shawna.

Martin had stayed with us but refrained from being his chatty self. I couldn't tell if the tension radiating from him was because he was anxious to fulfill his promise to me or an urgency to reach the spirit realm now that he'd reunited with Pete. Even the dog, who usually ran around smelling everything, seemed to be in a somber mood and paced alongside Martin.

Jade's mood wasn't much better. "What if we're too late and Hildie's already left?"

I'd been thinking the same thing. With Max removed as a suspect, I could have easily walked away and let the police handle the situation. Maybe even send them an anonymous tip suggesting they take a closer look at the murder weapon.

Unfortunately, this was no longer about solving a crime. Hildie had stolen from my family, taken a life, then staged the murder to implicate my uncle. "Hopefully, we're not." I forced my lips into a halfhearted smile. "I guess we can always regroup and come up with an alternative plan."

"I do nah believe that shall be necessary. Thar she be." Martin stopped right in front of me.

On instinct, I held up a hand as if bracing for impact and received an icy chill when it passed through his shoulder. "Where?" I shook my hand, trying to regain some warmth.

He tipped his head to the right. "She be headed toward yer witch friend's tent."

The tightness in my chest eased. "It looks like she's going to see Nadine," I told Jade as I switched directions.

"That's great." She sounded as nervous as I felt. "What should we do now?"

"I need to confront her, see if I can get her to admit the saber is Max's."

"Do you really think that's a good idea?" Jade kept her gaze focused on Hildie.

"No, but I don't think the police can do anything without…." The correct word eluded me, and I rubbed my forehead.

"Proof, probable cause, or something like that." Jade might not watch as many television crime shows as Shawna and I did, but was good with the terminology.

"Do me a favor and stay here." I glanced from Martin to Jade, making sure they knew I meant both of them.

"What? No." Concerned, Jade placed her hand on my arm. "I'm not letting you go by yourself."

"I'm afraid we'll spook her if we both show up." I gave her a reassuring pat, more for myself than for her. "I need you to send a text to Shawna and Bryce. Tell them where we're at and to bring Roy and Logan."

Jade frowned and reluctantly retrieved her phone. "And while I'm doing that, what are you going to do?"

"Distract her." I took a deep breath to steady my nerves and started walking.

If Hildie's plan was to act natural and avoid suspicion, she was doing a great job. I caught up with her when she got in line behind four people standing by the booth in front of Nadine's tent. Her costume looked a lot like Shawna's, but instead of a pistol, she had Martin's saber tucked into the leather scabbard secured around her waist.

Grams was selling tickets and noticed me immediately. She knew I'd do anything to keep from having my fortune read, so I waved, hoping it would soften her disbelieving scowl and keep her from asking any questions.

"Hey, Hildie." I ignored the uncomfortable knot in my stomach and focused on my task.

She startled, then quickly turned. "Oh, hello, Rylee." She appeared tense, but her smile didn't falter. "Any luck finding that eye patch you were looking for?"

"No, not yet. It turns out Max is more interested in swords." I let my gaze drop to the saber, and her entire body tensed.

"There you are." Jade appeared on my right, acting as if I hadn't asked her to wait for me. She probably had no idea Martin and Pete had followed her.

Being supportive in difficult situations was one of the many reasons she was my best friend. With Hildie being so jumpy, I wished she would have kept her distance. "Rylee was telling me you have some nice sword replicas. I was thinking about getting one for my brother." Her voice was laced with the same level of sweetness she used with customers at the shop.

"Oooh, is that one of them?" Jade pretended that she hadn't seen the saber until now. "Would you mind if I took a look at it?"

"Yes, I do mind," Hildie snapped and protectively curled her fingers around the hilt.

Now that the pleasantries were over, it was time to apply more pressure. "Would that be because it's really Martin Cumberpatch's saber and not a fake?" I clenched my fists. "Or because you stole it from my uncle?"

"How did you…" She took a step backward, then nervously glanced around.

173

People had taken notice of our conversation and were forming a large circle around us. Instead of bolting and pushing her way through the crowd as I'd expected, Hildie's dark eyes pinned me with an accusatory glare. "If anyone's to blame, it's Max. If he'd sold the saber back to me when I asked him to, then none of this would have happened."

"And what about Jake?" I asked. "Is he to blame too?"

"Yes," she hissed. "When I inherited the shop from my grandfather, I also ended up with all his debt. Jake offered to be a silent partner and help me out. Things weren't great, but I was making headway." Hildie stopped talking to stare at the ground as if she needed a moment to collect her thoughts.

"Not long after I got the saber from Clyde, I found out it belonged to Martin Cumberpatch. I'd even found a buyer who was willing to give me a lot of money for it." She sighed. "It would have been enough to pay Jake what I owed him to get out of the partnership and make sure I never had any more financial problems with the shop."

Grams appeared on the other side of Jade. She looked fiercer than a mother bear protecting her cubs, and I knew keeping her out of the conversation was moot. "If you knew the blade was valuable, then why sell it to my son in the first place?"

"I didn't." Hildie's voice got considerably louder. "One of my employees found it in the storeroom and sold it to Max while I was in Portland attending an auction."

"If swapping out the blades was going to solve your problems, then why get rid of Jake?" I asked.

Hildie pursed her lips and snarled, "Somehow, he found out about the blade's origins and told me if I didn't pay him what I owed him plus half of what I got from the sale he'd make sure I lost the shop."

Martin snickered. "Sounds like the bloke got wha' he deserved then."

"Not helping," I muttered.

Jade's sidelong glance went from me to the cell she'd been hiding in the ruffled folds of her short skirt. She took a half step forward, then slid her arm behind her back so I could see the screen.

She must have changed the phone's settings to vibrate because I hadn't heard it ring. Shawna had returned Jade's text, the message stating that help was on the way in capped and bolded letters. I assumed the skull and crossbones emojis before and after the words had to be Nate's doing.

Unless I wanted to tackle Hildie to the ground to stop her from leaving before Roy arrived, I needed to keep her talking. "Was Braden helping you? Is that why you hid the saber on the *Sea Witch*?"

"No, he didn't know anything about my relationship with Jake." Disdain laced her voice. "Braden despised him as much as I did, only he'd found a way to get out of their partnership without having his finances ruined."

If Hildie was right about Braden, it might explain the call Martin had overheard. "Then why hide the blade on Jake's boat?" I asked.

"You mean besides wanting to enjoy the irony." Hildie's gaze darkened, and she sneered. "Someone carrying a sword that late at night would have been noticed, and I needed to blend in with the tourists."

Roy picked that moment to make his way through the wall of people with Elliott, Nate, and Shawna following closely behind him. Knowing my friend, I was certain she'd filled the sheriff in on every detail about what we'd discovered. Everything that didn't include Martin's participation and the fact that I could see ghosts.

Roy motioned for them to stay back with the rest of the crowd as he took a few steps closer to Hildie. "I understand we might have a situation here." His deep voice and the laid-back way he carried himself usually put people at ease.

Hildie wasn't one of those people. She slid the saber

from her belt at the same time she spun around to face him.

"Don't come any closer." She gripped the blade with both hands and swiped it back and forth through the air.

"Hildie, why don't you put that down so we can talk?" Roy holding up his hands and motioning for her to lower the saber seemed to upset her even more.

She growled and swung the blade toward anything that moved. People gasped, others murmured, and at least one person shrieked.

Grams leaned toward me. "It looks like Roy could use some help."

I tucked my arm through hers when she started forward. There was no way I was letting my grandmother get close to a crazy woman wielding a blade. "Maybe he's waiting for Logan."

I'd been too busy wrangling Grams to notice that Martin had vanished and reappeared behind Hildie. I knew what was coming next and waved my free hand, then shouted, "No, wait," before I could stop myself.

Not that it mattered or stopped Martin from wrenching the saber out of Hildie's hands. The frosty zap of warm skin touching a spirit, something I'd experienced a few times, along with losing control of her weapon, had Hildie screaming hysterically.

Martin wasted no time in walking toward me and placing the sword on the ground near my feet. To me, his actions appeared normal, but to the rest of the onlookers, it probably looked like the blade had levitated all by itself.

"You be welcome," he said before I could utter a single scolding word. After tugging on the brim of his hat, he placed his hand on Pete's head, then did what he did best—disappear.

Roy's shocked reaction to what had happened didn't last long. He'd grown up in Cumberpatch, and in his line of work, had probably seen more unexplainable things than I cared to think about.

176

Within minutes, he had Hildie handcuffed and turned over to Elliott. Shortly after that, more police officers arrived, the crowd was dispersed, and things seemed to go back to normal. Or at least as normal as they were going to get until someone started screeching like a banshee and shouted, "I told you she was a witch." I knew before I spun around that the shrill female voice belonged to Trudy. She was clutching Lavender's arm and frantically jabbing a finger in my direction, trying to get the attention of anyone who would listen.

Grams and Jade had turned with me, but it was my grandmother who came to my defense first. "I suggest you stop telling everybody my granddaughter is a witch; otherwise, you might find yourself transformed into a frog." She snickered when Lavender paled, grabbed her cousin by the arm, and practically dragged her from the area.

"Nice one." Shawna strolled over and did a high-five with Grams. "I especially liked the frog part."

"Unbelievable." I threw my hands in the air. "Now, everyone in town is going to think I can cast spells." I glared at Shawna. "And what is it with you and frogs?" I hadn't expected an answer, but I knew the smirk was coming.

Jade draped her arm around my shoulder. "Look on the bright side."

I was having a hard time imagining anything sparkly, enlightening, or positive to come out of the current situation. "Which is?"

"Your secret about seeing ghosts is still safe."

***

With nothing more to see, things settled down rather quickly. The few remaining onlookers lost interest and returned to enjoying the festivities. Bryce and Myra had arrived shortly after Hildie was being helped into the back of a police cruiser.

I'd already explained to Nate why Trudy thought I was a witch. I wasn't in the mood for another lengthy conversation, so Jade pulled them off to the side to fill them in on what they'd missed. Grams had returned to help Nadine, but not before calling Max. Even though he couldn't see her, the details she'd given him included dramatic arm movements.

Troy showed up armed with a camera he'd been using to take pictures of the festival. My friends and I had refused to give him any comments, so he'd cornered Nate for an interview. Nate had been talking non-stop for the last few minutes, excited his information would be quoted in tomorrow's headline article.

"I'll bet Max will be glad to get this back." Shawna walked toward me after picking up the saber Martin left on the ground before he'd disappeared. Though I wasn't usually a spiteful person, I'd been pondering the ways I could get even with the ghost for causing so much chaos to worry about retrieving it. The only thing making me feel better was knowing he'd helped my friends and I find Hildie.

After what happened the last time I'd touched the blade, I refused to take it when she held it out to me. "Maybe you should check with Roy and see if he needs it for evidence or something."

"That's a good idea." She hurried off to where Roy was standing and talking to Elliott.

Now that I was by myself, I closed my eyes, took a deep breath, and enjoyed my solitude.

"Rylee." As always, my stomach fluttered at the sound of Logan's deep voice.

"Yes." I opened my eyes, then braced for a lecture as I turned to face him. He stood a couple of feet away from me, his intense gaze filled with concern rather than irritation. At a distance, he'd looked great in his pirate outfit, but up close, he was even more handsome.

"Roy called and said you had a run-in with Jake's killer. Are you all right?"

"I'm fine and totally unscathed." I smiled. "Thanks for asking."

"I would've been here sooner, but I got held up by Edith and Joyce Haverston."

I wondered if they'd shared one of their obscure predictions with him. "Do I want to know why?"

He shook his head. "No, but I'm curious about something."

"Which is?"

"How did you know Hildie had the saber?" Logan asked.

"Would you believe me if I told you I had some ghostly help?" I wanted to gauge his reaction and tried for honesty first.

"I rely on facts and things I can actually see to do my job, so I'd have to say probably not." He tweaked the fabric below the knot on my cap. "Although, since moving here, I've seen a few things I can't explain."

His admission was progress and gave me hope that someday he'd be open to hearing about my paranormal ability. Until then, I planned to avoid the topic and scrambled for a reason he'd believe, one based on truth no matter how slim.

Josh picked that moment to interrupt. "Rylee, there you are. I've been looking all over for you." He'd solved my explanation problem but had created a new one.

He must have gone home to change after his encounter with Martin because he'd exchanged a tan pair of pants made from a stretchy material for the striped ones I'd seen him wearing earlier.

"Come on." He ignored Logan as if he wasn't standing right in front of me, then took my hand. "If we don't leave now, we'll miss registration for the couple's costume contest."

"What?" I yanked my hand free. "I'm not doing any

contest with you or anyone else."

"But you're my girlfriend and you…"

It was painful to see a grown man pout. I'd already had a rough day and surpassed my limit for being understanding. If Josh's interruption wasn't ruining my time with Logan, I might have been more sympathetic. I held up my hand when he reached for my wrist again. "Josh, you're a nice guy, and I don't want to hurt your feelings, but I'm *not* your girlfriend, *nor* will I ever be."

He shook his head, unwilling to listen. "I know you don't mean that." He was a foot shorter than Logan and should have been intimidated, yet he tried to wedge himself between us. "I guess it's okay if you don't want to do the contest. We can do something else."

Logan had been watching our interaction, his expression a combination of curiosity and amusement. He must've noticed me clenching my fists and decided to intervene. "I believe the lady said she wasn't interested. Maybe you should back away and leave her alone."

Josh blinked and glared at Logan. "Look, whoever you are, she happens to be my girlfriend, so you need to mind your own business." He puffed out his chest and gripped the hilt of the fake sword tucked inside his belt.

With Logan dressed as a pirate, Josh had no idea he was a police detective. He also must not have known he was Roy's nephew. If he had, he would have taken off running, and they wouldn't be having this conversation. "Josh, this is Logan and he…"

"Rylee, is it true?" Logan cut me off, his dark eyes glinting with mischief. "Are ye this bloke's girlfriend?"

Bloke? It wasn't uncommon for the locals to get into role-playing during the festival, but I hadn't expected it from Logan. Deciding to go along, I feigned a heavy sigh. "No, he be mistaken."

Logan took a few steps back and drew his sword. "Then I 'ave no choice but to defend yer honor." He challenged Josh by swiping his blade near his chest.

Josh's eyes gleamed. "Then prepare fer defeat." He tugged on his own sword, the blade catching on his belt, the movement less graceful then Logan's had been.

"Guys, you really don't need to do this." When Logan drew his sword, I'd assumed he wanted to warn Josh off, not provoke him into a duel. I had to admit I was shocked, if not a little flattered, by the old-fashioned display.

They glared at me as if I'd insulted them. "Okay, then." I held up my hands and backed away just as the clank of metal filled the air. The swords they used were made from stainless steel, not the harmless plastic versions sold in the children's section of my family's shop. I doubted the imitations were capable of ending anyone's life, but they'd sting if they connected with flesh.

They exchanged verbal barbs as they parried back and forth. It was like watching a swashbuckler movie; the only thing missing was having the battle take place on a real pirate ship.

People strolling nearby got out of the way to give Josh and Logan room, then stayed to watch what they presumed was part of the festivities. It didn't take long for the crowd to grow. Even Roy, Elliott, and the spoofers gathered to cheer and give Logan their support.

Josh wasn't a novice when it came to wielding a sword. Mattie told me more than once how he liked to spend a lot of time in the swordplay area when he visited. What surprised me the most was how adept and graceful Logan handled his blade.

"Geez, we leave you alone for a few minutes and look what happens," Shawna said as she and Jade walked up beside me.

They'd been sharing a bag of cotton candy, the evidence on their matching blue tongues.

"Yep, she's a regular trouble magnet." Jade held the half-empty bag out to me.

Sweets were my weakness, and I didn't hesitate to snatch a handful of the fluffed sugar.

"Wow, Logan has great form," Shawna said.

I gave him an admiring glance. "Yes, he does."

Jade laughed and gave my arm a light smack. "I think she was talking about his fighting abilities."

I stuffed the candy in my mouth, then licked my sticky fingers. "So was I." Sort of. Logan was a hot guy, so who could blame me for ogling? Having someone willing to fight for my honor wasn't an everyday occurrence, and I planned to enjoy it while it lasted.

"If Josh wins, does that mean you have to start dating him?" Shawna waved a lump of candy in front of my face and giggled.

"Not likely." I snatched the sugary sweetness out of her hand.

"Hey," she grumbled, then reached inside the bag for another piece.

"I don't think it's going to be a problem." Jade tipped her chin toward the waning duel.

While Logan looked as if he'd barely started to sweat, Josh was wheezing, his swings slow and halfhearted. Logan's next swipe knocked the sword out of Josh's hand and sent the blade sailing through the air. It landed on the pavement with a clatter.

Logan lowered his sword. "I believe I win unless you're interested in continuing."

"Fine." Josh dragged his feet as he walked over to retrieve his blade. "No girl is worth this much effort." He scowled at me, then headed for a gap in the crowd.

"Oh, I don't know about that." Logan glanced in my direction, his smile causing heat to rush to my cheeks.

"You need to congratulate the winner." Jade gave me a nudge toward Logan.

I wasn't graceful and was glad I'd reached him without stumbling. "That was quite a demonstration." I noticed my blue fingertips and tucked my hands in my pockets. There wasn't anything I could do about the color of my tongue and was happy he didn't mention it. "Where did you learn to fight so well?"

"I've participated in a few renaissance fairs." He slipped his sword back into his belt. "Though I'm much better at jousting."

He never seemed to lack confidence when he was around me, and I'd bet there were quite a few things he was good at. "Thank you for protecting my honor and for helping me out with Josh."

"You're more than welcome, though I did have an ulterior motive." He took my hand and pulled me closer.

I placed my hands on his chest. "And what would that be?" My heart raced, and the flutters were back.

He grinned and lowered his head. "To collect the kiss a lady bestows on her champion."

CHAPTER TWENTY-ONE

The sun had started to set, and brilliant stripes of pink and gold filled the early evening sky. With fall closely approaching, it wouldn't be long before the daily temperatures dropped, and every day would require warmer clothes and jackets.

I sat on the blanket Jade and I placed on the sand next to the fire Bryce and Nate built shortly after our group had arrived on the beach. After reading the article in the newspaper about the pirate ship sighting, Bryce had pestered my friends and me to accompany him and check it out. He thought my special ghostly ability might make the ship reappear. Since we hadn't participated in a campfire outing in a long time, we agreed to go along and make a night of it.

I stared at the flames glad that Hildie had been caught and the festival was over. The second day of activities hadn't seemed nearly as exciting as the first. Not when I thought about the wonderful kiss I'd gotten from Logan.

Shawna discovered her future didn't hold anything exciting but was happy she'd gotten her reading from Nadine. I hadn't seen Martin and Pete since the Trudy episode, yet somehow sensed their trip to the afterlife had been postponed. Even so, I didn't think a trip to the cove would magically produce them or a glimpse of the vessel the spoofers were hoping for.

"Have you seen anything yet?" Shawna asked as soon as she returned from her walk with Nate.

"Nothing so far." I scooted closer to Jade to make room for them to sit on the other half of the blanket.

"That's too bad." Nate reached into a nearby food basket and pulled out a bag of marshmallows and two metal roasting prongs, then handed one to Shawna. "We've spent a few nights out here watching and were hoping we'd actually see something this time."

I glanced at Bryce and Myra, who were standing near the water's edge staring at the rippling waves. I'd been afraid to ask where he'd gotten the night vision goggles or what he expected to see with them.

"It's still early." Shawna sounded confident. "Maybe the witching hour rules also apply to pirate ships." She grabbed a handful of marshmallows, then stuffed one in her mouth and stuck the other two on the end of her stick.

"I hadn't thought about that." Nate finished squishing as many marshmallows as possible on his prong, then held it over the fire. "You'll have to mention it to Bryce and Myra when they come back."

Jade and I remained silent. She didn't agree with Shawna's theory any more than I did, but unlike me, she chose to show her skepticism with a roll of her eyes.

There wasn't a breeze, yet cool air broke through the fires warmth and swirled around me. For the first time since I'd started getting ghostly visits, I welcomed the chill. I stretched and got to my feet seconds before Martin and Pete made an appearance.

"Hey, Martin," I said so my friends would know he'd arrived. Jade, Shawna, and Nate stopped what they were doing. If I'd known they were going to stare, I would have taken a walk so I could talk to him privately. Since it was too late, I did my best to ignore them.

"Evening, Lass." As soon as he scratched Pete's head, the dog sat on the ground next to him, body pressed against his leg, tail wagging. Pete still had a bandanna tied around his neck, but Martin had changed into the pirate outfit he'd worn the first day we met. "I suppose ye know why I be here?"

I did, but I didn't want to admit it, so I teased him instead. "Let me guess, you came to tell me you drenched someone else with a soda."

He chortled. "Ye will be thankin' me later. The good detective be smitten wit' ye 'n be a much better match than that Josh fellow."

"I suppose you're right." I felt the evening chill now that I'd moved away from the fire and pulled my jacket closer to my chest.

His grin faded, and he rubbed his hand along his nape. "Rylee, 'tis time fer me 'n Pete to be on our way, so I 'ave come to say goodbye."

"Oh." Even though I knew it was time and had been prepared, it didn't prevent my chest from tightening.

"Ye 'ave been a good friend to us 'n I be goin' to miss ye." His voice cracked, and Pete whimpered.

"I'll miss you too." I blinked away the moisture building in my eyes. "I'd give you a hug if it wouldn't turn me into a block of ice."

"'n I would let ye." Martin winked. "Ye take care of yourself."

"I will." I watched the two of them fade, then vanish completely.

Jade and Shawna had gotten to their feet, and as soon as I told them Martin was gone, they pulled me into a group hug.

"The spirit world will never be the same." Shawna stepped away from me and held out her roasting prong, offering me the remaining burnt marshmallow.

"That's for sure." I pulled on the sticky blob, then popped it into my mouth, and followed my friends back to the blanket. I was about to take my seat when movement on the water caught my attention. "Well, I'll be darned."

Jade followed the direction of my gaze. "Did you see something?"

I debated whether or not I should tell my friends about the glimpse I'd gotten of a pirate ship, or that Martin was standing on the deck with Pete beside him, his front paws hooked on the railing.

I shook my head and grinned. "Nope, just a reflection."

Even though I knew he was headed for the spirit realm, I couldn't shake the feeling I'd be seeing the wayward pirate and his best mate again someday.

ABOUT THE AUTHOR

Nola Robertson is an author of paranormal and sci-fi romance, who has recently ventured into writing cozy mysteries. When she's not busy writing, she spends her time reading, gardening, and working on various DIY projects.

Raised in the Midwest, she now resides in the enchanting Southwest with her husband and three adorable cats.

Made in the USA
Monee, IL
14 December 2020

53219617R00114